LUKE SKYWALKER AND THE
TREASURE OF THE DRAGONSNAKES

visit us at www.abdopublishing.com

Reinforced library bound edition published in 2012 by Spotlight, a division of the ABDO Group, 8000 West 78th Street, Edina, Minnesota 55439.
Spotlight produces high-quality reinforced library bound editions for schools and libraries. Published by agreement with Dark Horse Comics, Inc., and Lucasfilm Ltd.
Printed in the United States of America, Melrose Park, Illinois.
052010
092010
This book contains at least 10% recycled materials.

Special thanks to Elaine Mederer, Jann Moorhead, David Anderman, Leland Chee, Sue Rostoni, and Carol Roeder at Lucas Licensing

Cataloging-in-Publication Data

Taylor, Tom.
Star wars adventures: Luke Skywalker and the treasure of the dragonsnakes /
   script Tom Taylor ; art Daxiong ; lettering Michael Heisler ; cover art Daxiong.
-- Reinforced library bound ed.
   p. cm. -- (Star Wars Adventures)
1. Star Wars fiction. 2. Science fiction comic books, strips, etc.
3. Young adult fiction. I. Daxiong. II. Heisler, Michael. III. Title.
[741.5]--dc22

ISBN 978-1-59961-901-9 (reinforced library bound edition)

All Spotlight books are reinforced library bindings
and manufactured in the United States of America.

LUKE SKYWALKER AND THE
TREASURE OF THE DRAGONSNAKES

3 1389 02074 7382

Script **Tom Taylor**

Art **Daxiong**

Lettering **Michael Heisler**

Cover art **Daxiong**

Dark Horse Books®

THIS STORY TAKES PLACE DURING
STAR WARS: THE EMPIRE STRIKES BACK.

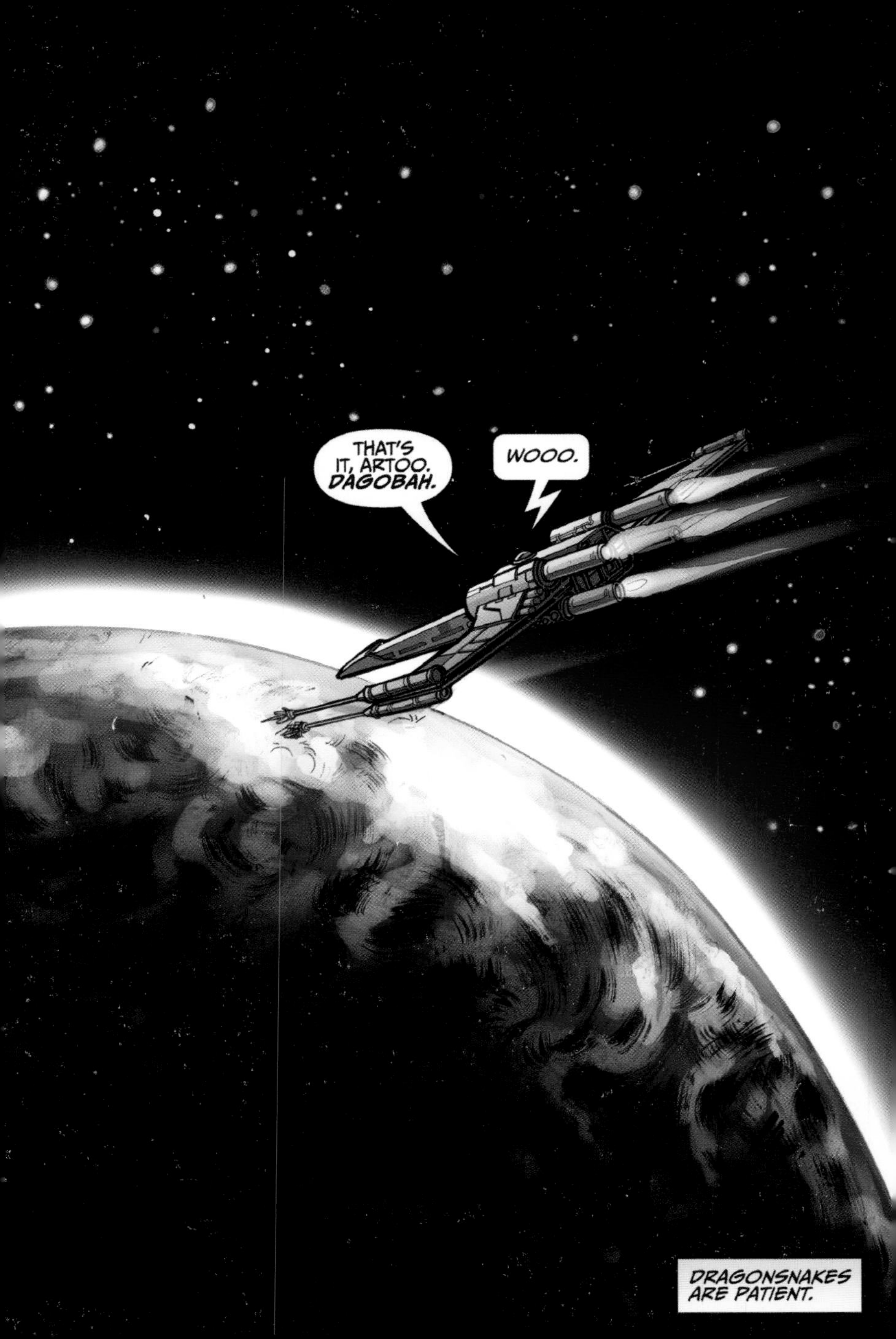

THAT'S IT, ARTOO. DAGOBAH.
WOOO.
DRAGONSNAKES ARE PATIENT.

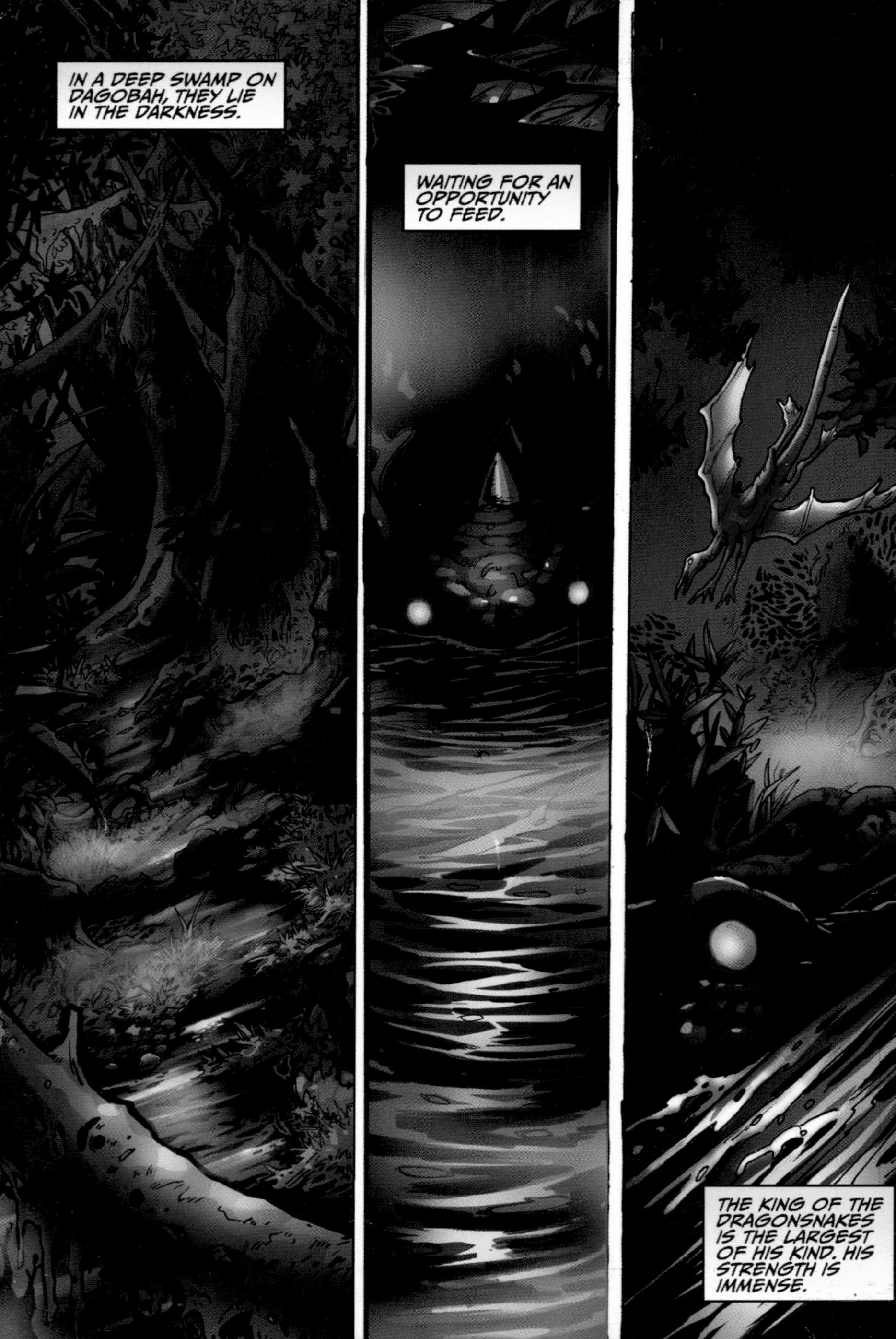
IN A DEEP SWAMP ON DAGOBAH, THEY LIE IN THE DARKNESS.
WAITING FOR AN OPPORTUNITY TO FEED.
THE KING OF THE DRAGONSNAKES IS THE LARGEST OF HIS KIND. HIS STRENGTH IS IMMENSE.

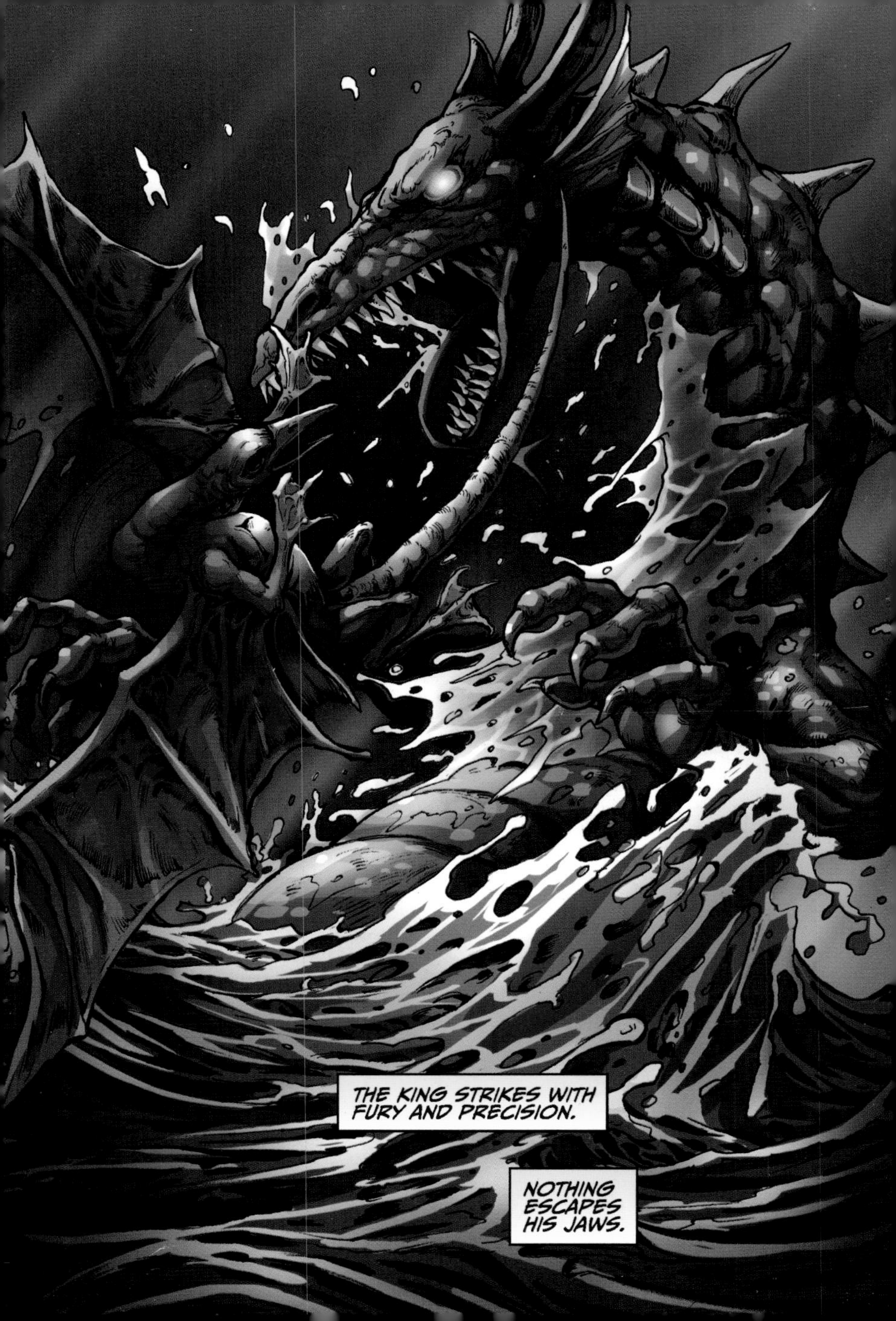
THE KING STRIKES WITH FURY AND PRECISION.
NOTHING ESCAPES HIS JAWS.

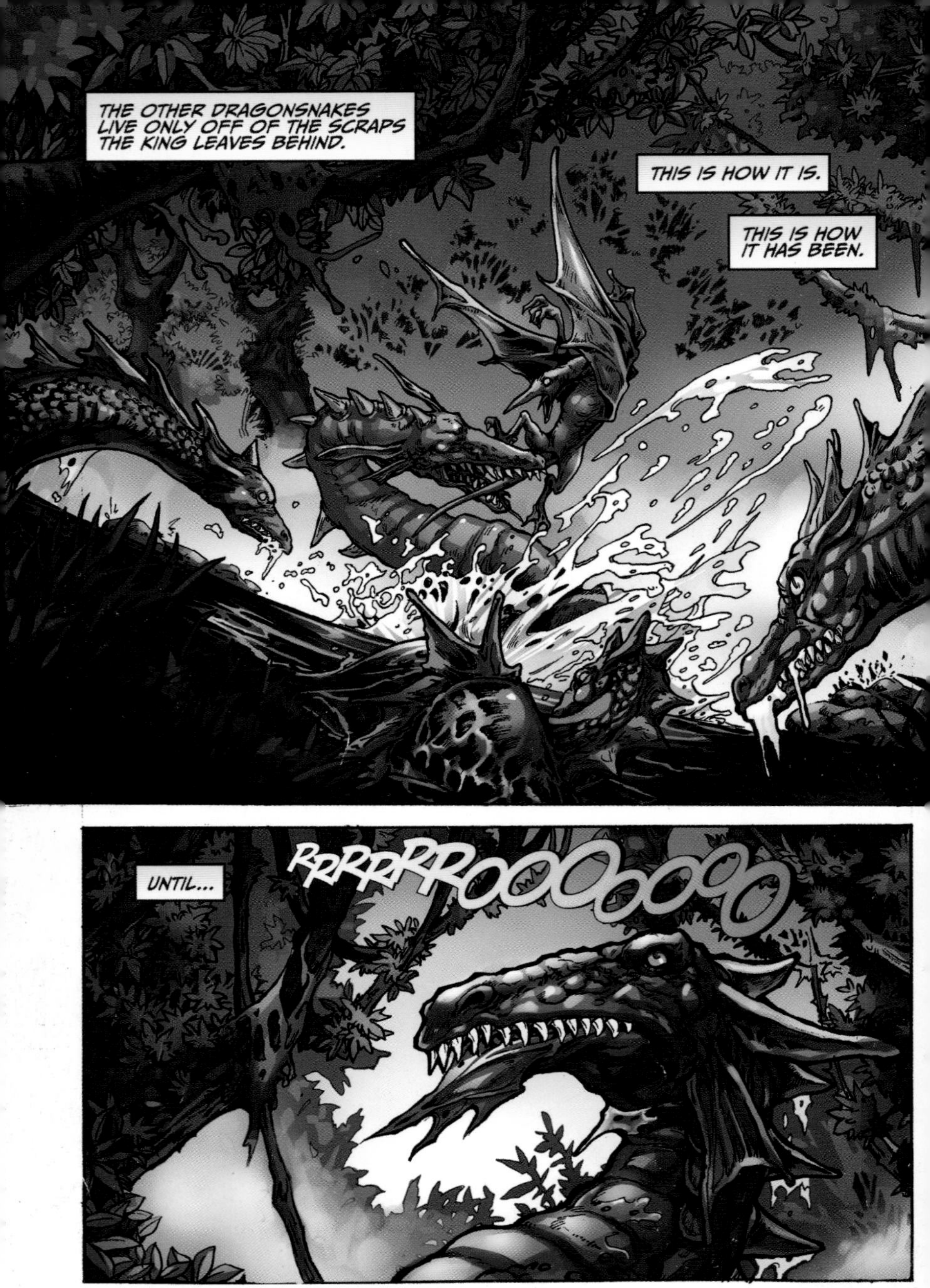
THE OTHER DRAGONSNAKES LIVE ONLY OFF OF THE SCRAPS THE KING LEAVES BEHIND.
THIS IS HOW IT IS.
THIS IS HOW IT HAS BEEN.
UNTIL...
RRRRRROOOOOOOO

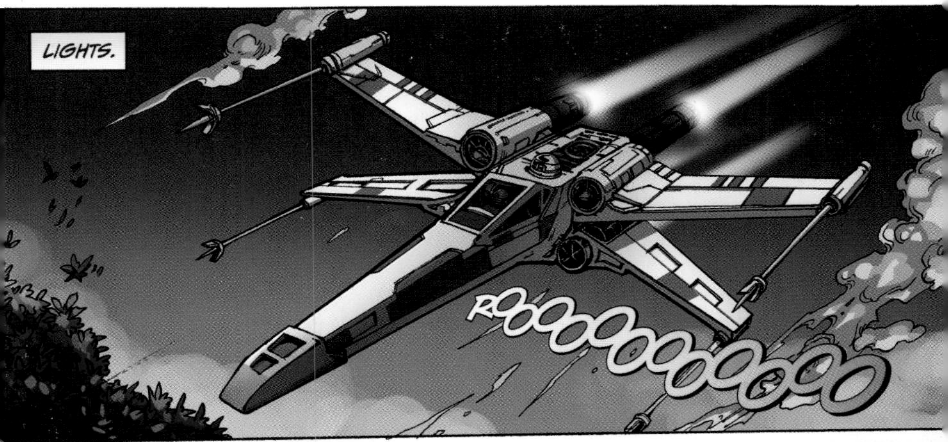
LIGHTS.
ROOOOOOOOOOOO

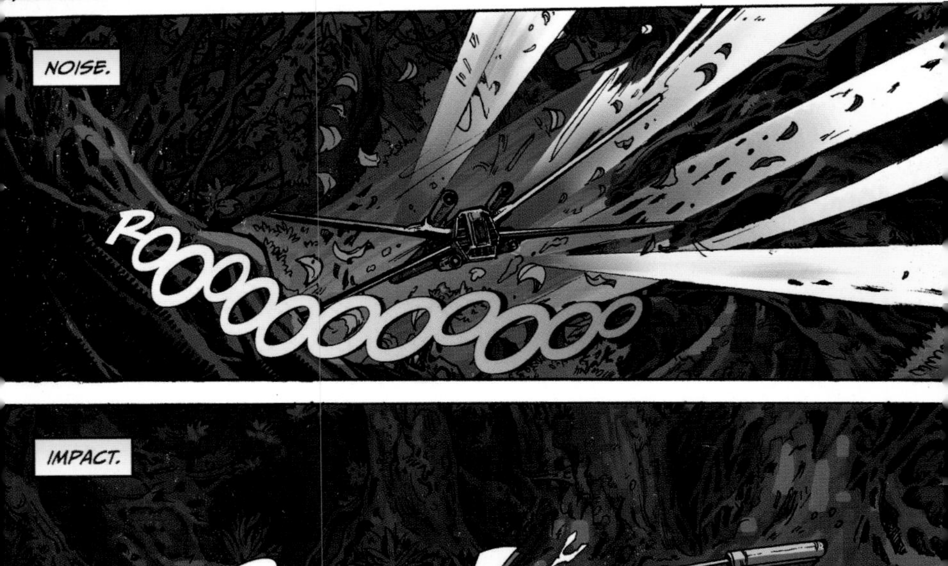
NOISE.
ROOOOOOOOOOOOO

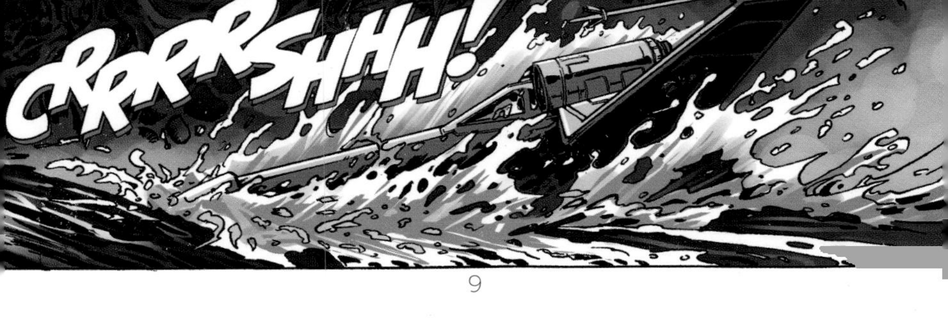
IMPACT.
CRRRRSHHH!

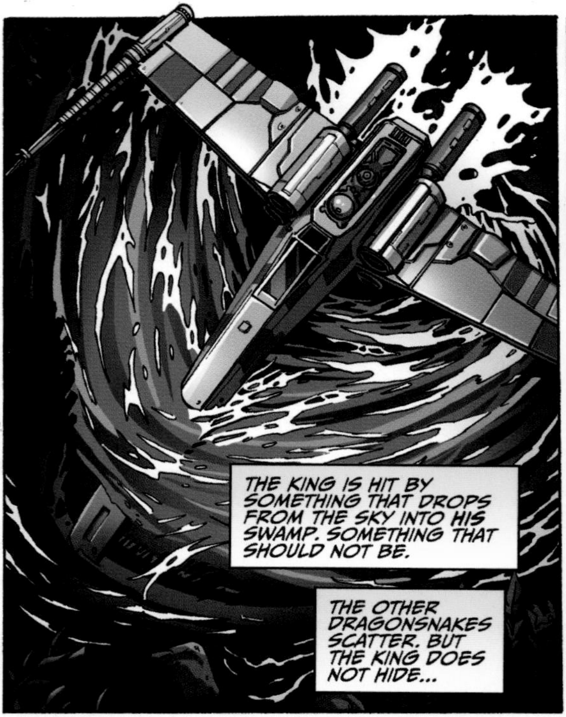
THE KING IS HIT BY SOMETHING THAT DROPS FROM THE SKY INTO HIS SWAMP. SOMETHING THAT SHOULD NOT BE.
THE OTHER DRAGONSNAKES SCATTER. BUT THE KING DOES NOT HIDE...

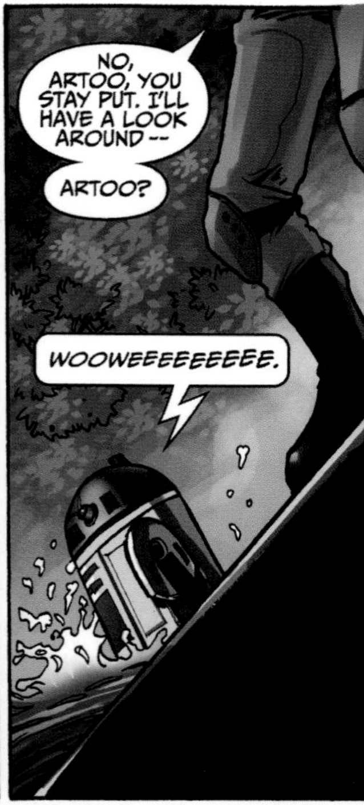
NO, ARTOO, YOU STAY PUT. I'LL HAVE A LOOK AROUND --
ARTOO?
WOOWEEEEEEEEEE.

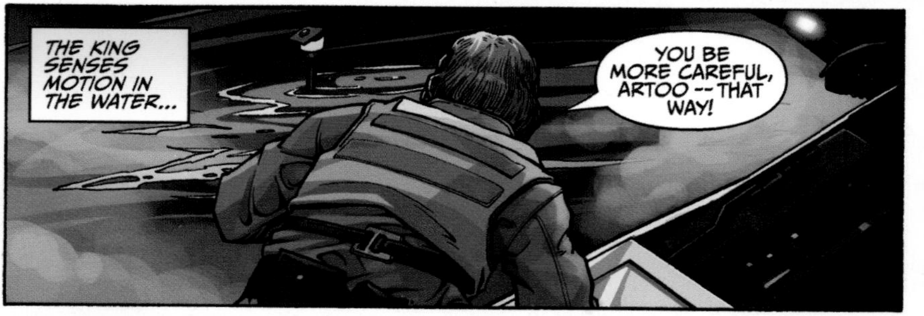
THE KING SENSES MOTION IN THE WATER...
YOU BE MORE CAREFUL, ARTOO -- THAT WAY!

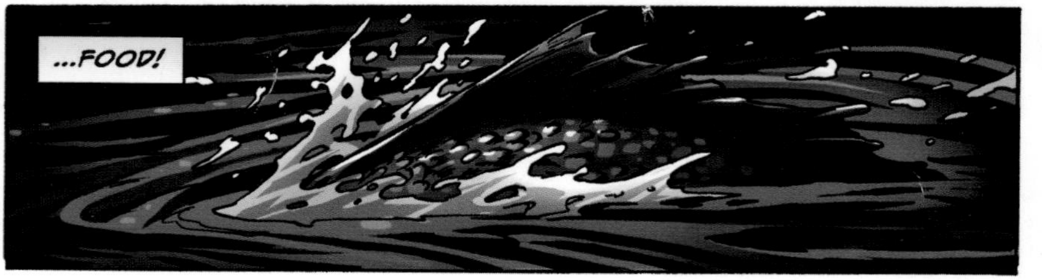
...FOOD!

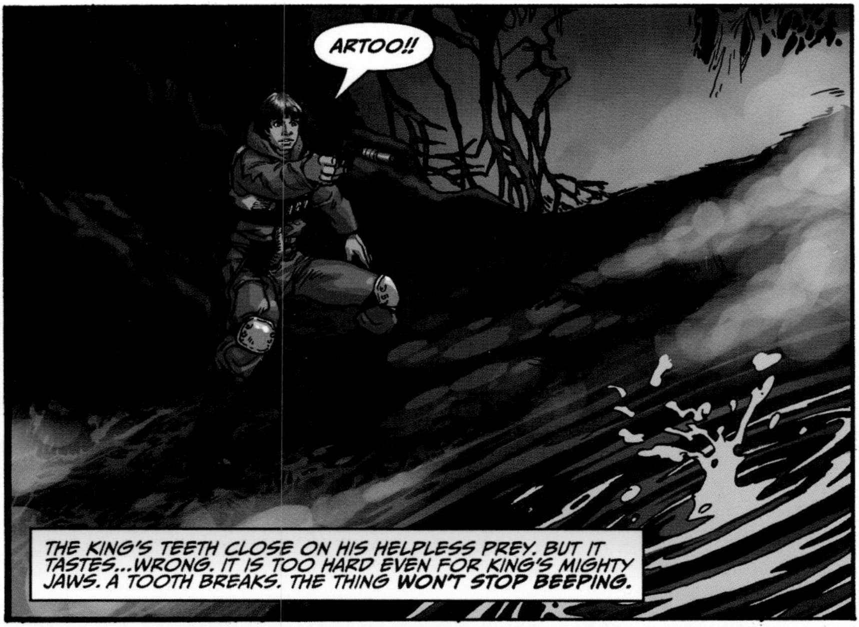
ARTOO!!
THE KING'S TEETH CLOSE ON HIS HELPLESS PREY. BUT IT TASTES...WRONG. IT IS TOO HARD EVEN FOR KING'S MIGHTY JAWS. A TOOTH BREAKS. THE THING WON'T STOP BEEPING.

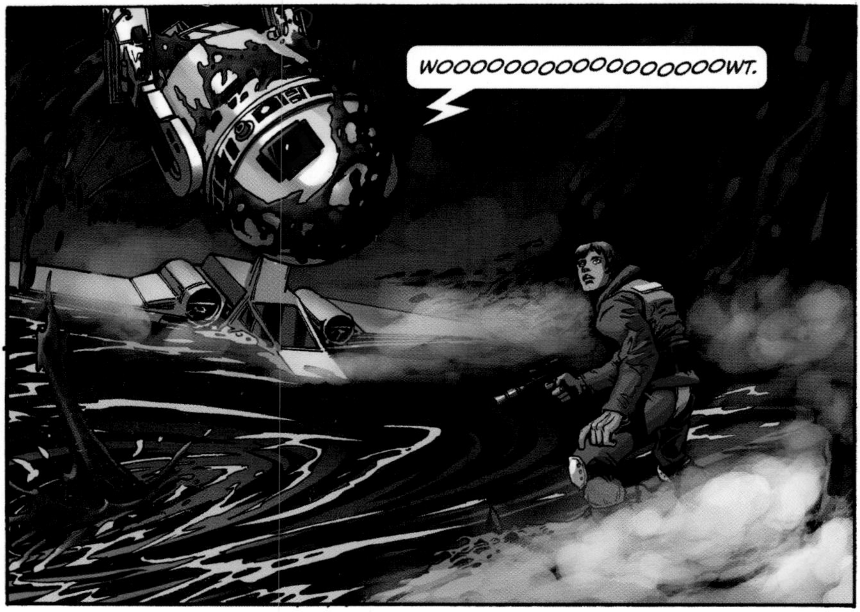
WOOOOOOOOOOOOOOOOOOWT.

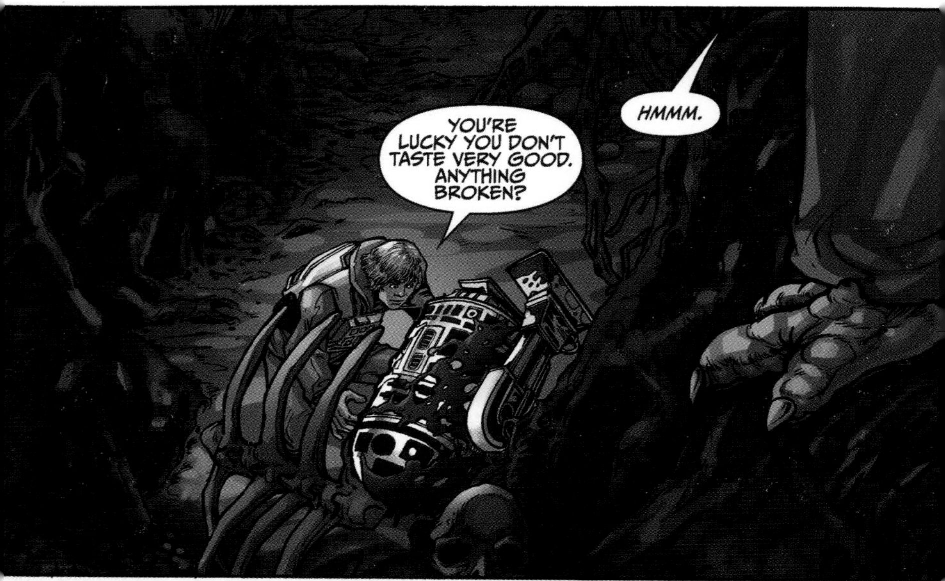
YOU'RE LUCKY YOU DON'T TASTE VERY GOOD. ANYTHING BROKEN?
HMMM.

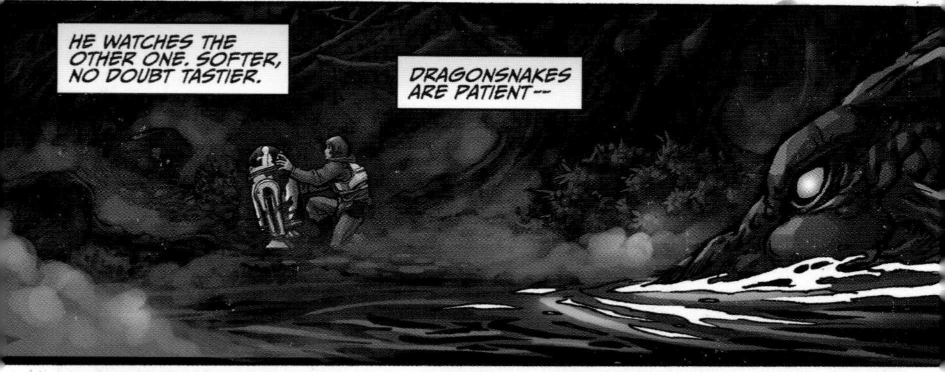
HE WATCHES THE OTHER ONE. SOFTER, NO DOUBT TASTIER.
DRAGONSNAKES ARE PATIENT--

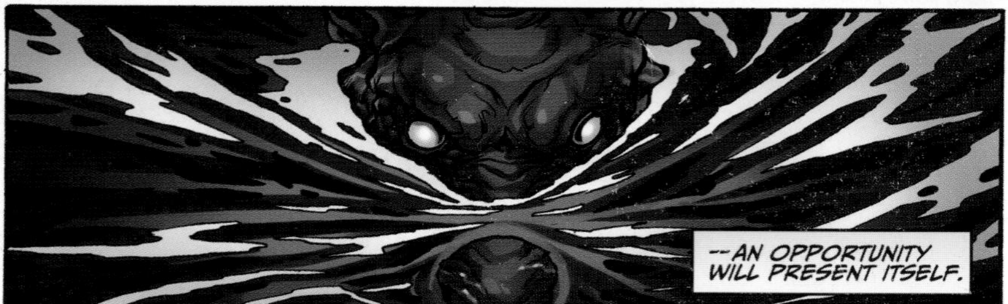
--AN OPPORTUNITY WILL PRESENT ITSELF.

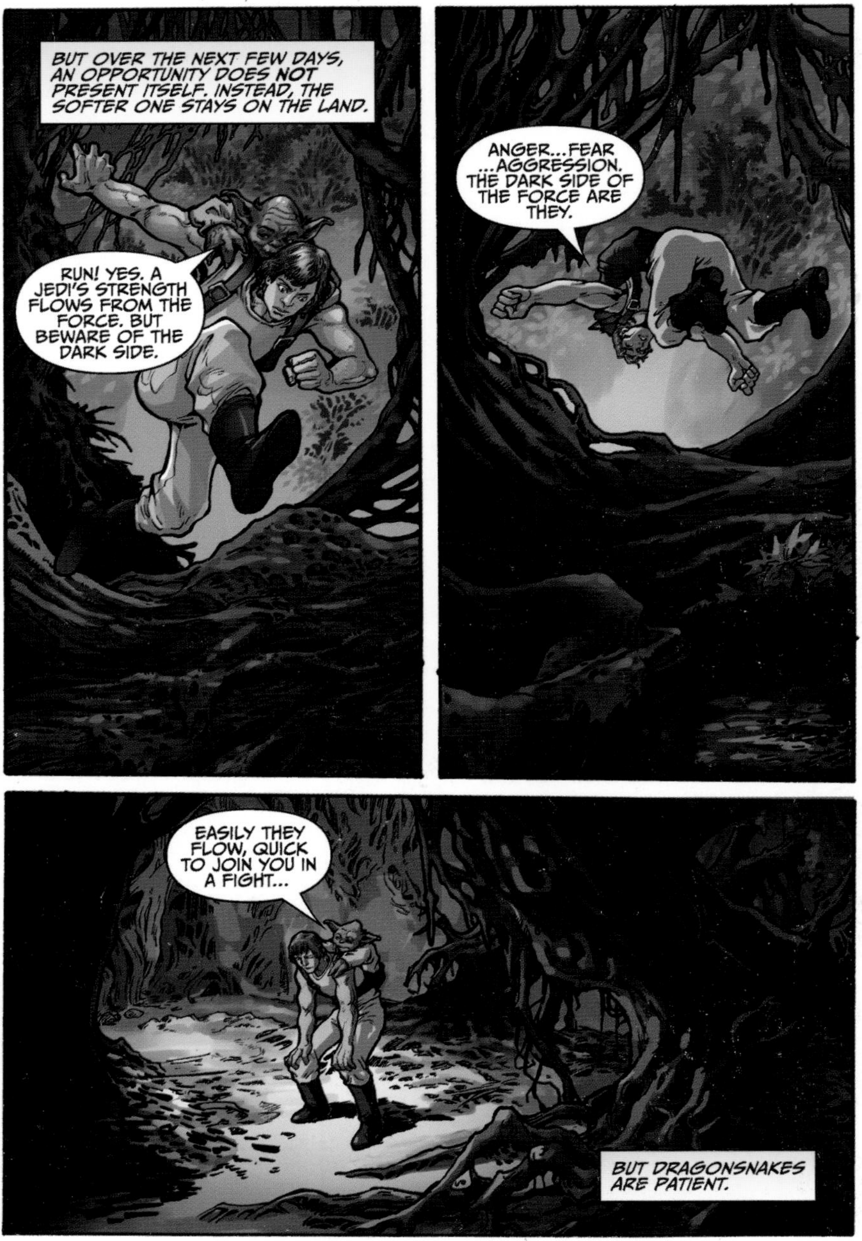
BUT OVER THE NEXT FEW DAYS, AN OPPORTUNITY DOES NOT PRESENT ITSELF. INSTEAD, THE SOFTER ONE STAYS ON THE LAND.
RUN! YES. A JEDI'S STRENGTH FLOWS FROM THE FORCE. BUT BEWARE OF THE DARK SIDE.
ANGER...FEAR ...AGGRESSION. THE DARK SIDE OF THE FORCE ARE THEY.
EASILY THEY FLOW, QUICK TO JOIN YOU IN A FIGHT...
BUT DRAGONSNAKES ARE PATIENT.

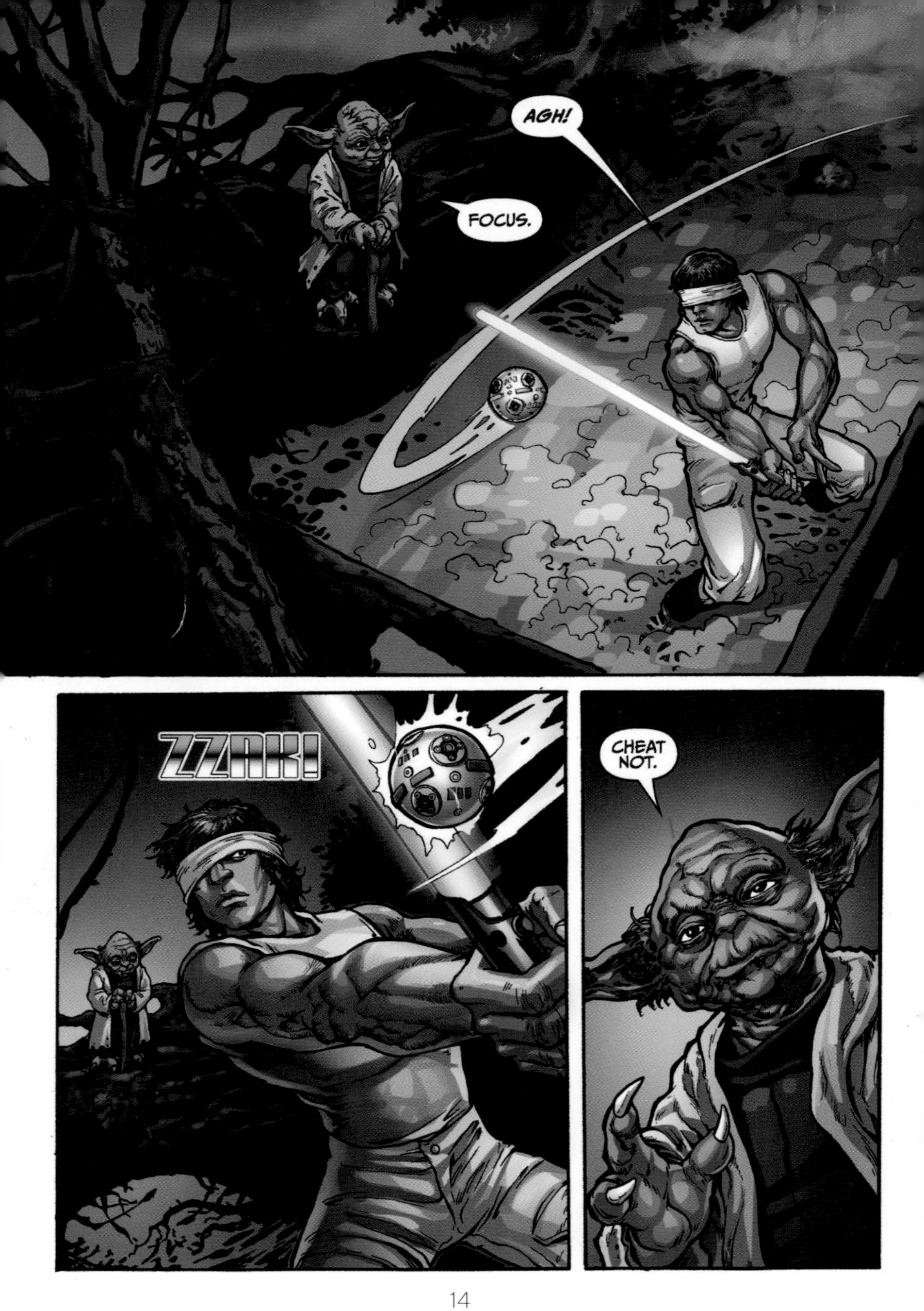
FOCUS.
AGH!
ZZAK!
CHEAT NOT.

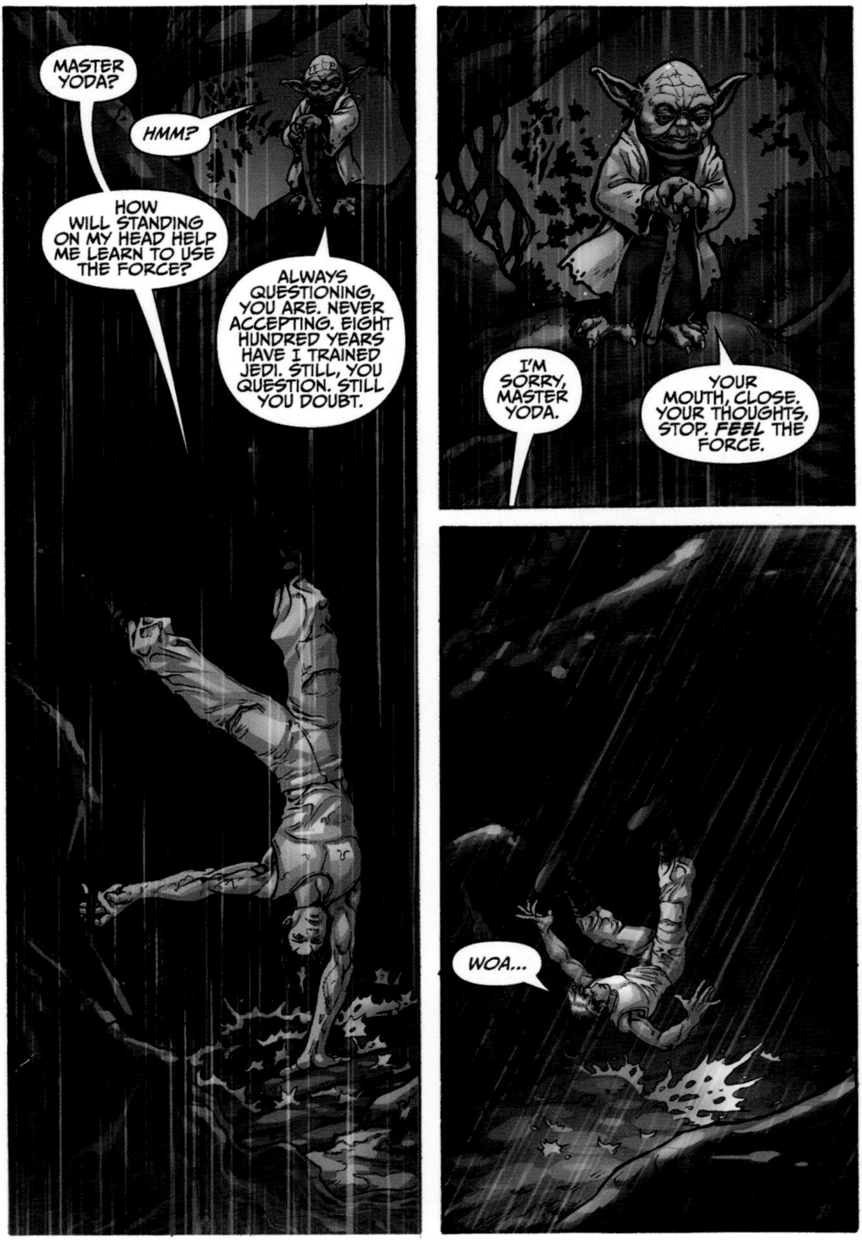
MASTER YODA?
HMM?
HOW WILL STANDING ON MY HEAD HELP ME LEARN TO USE THE FORCE?
ALWAYS QUESTIONING, YOU ARE. NEVER ACCEPTING. EIGHT HUNDRED YEARS HAVE I TRAINED JEDI. STILL, YOU QUESTION. STILL YOU DOUBT.
I'M SORRY, MASTER YODA.
YOUR MOUTH, CLOSE. YOUR THOUGHTS, STOP. FEEL THE FORCE.
WOA...

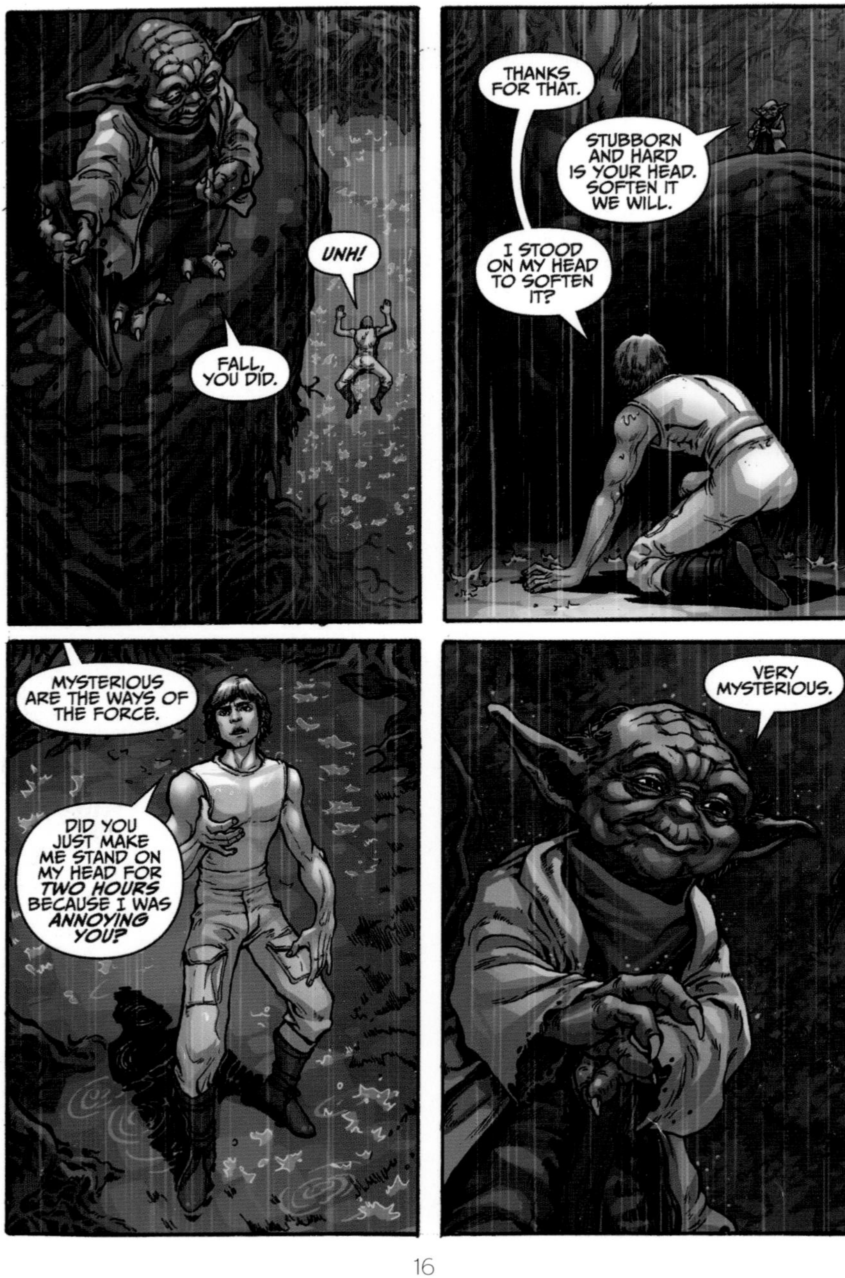
UNH!
FALL, YOU DID.
THANKS FOR THAT.
STUBBORN AND HARD IS YOUR HEAD. SOFTEN IT WE WILL.
I STOOD ON MY HEAD TO SOFTEN IT?
MYSTERIOUS ARE THE WAYS OF THE FORCE.
DID YOU JUST MAKE ME STAND ON MY HEAD FOR *TWO HOURS* BECAUSE I WAS *ANNOYING* YOU?
VERY MYSTERIOUS.

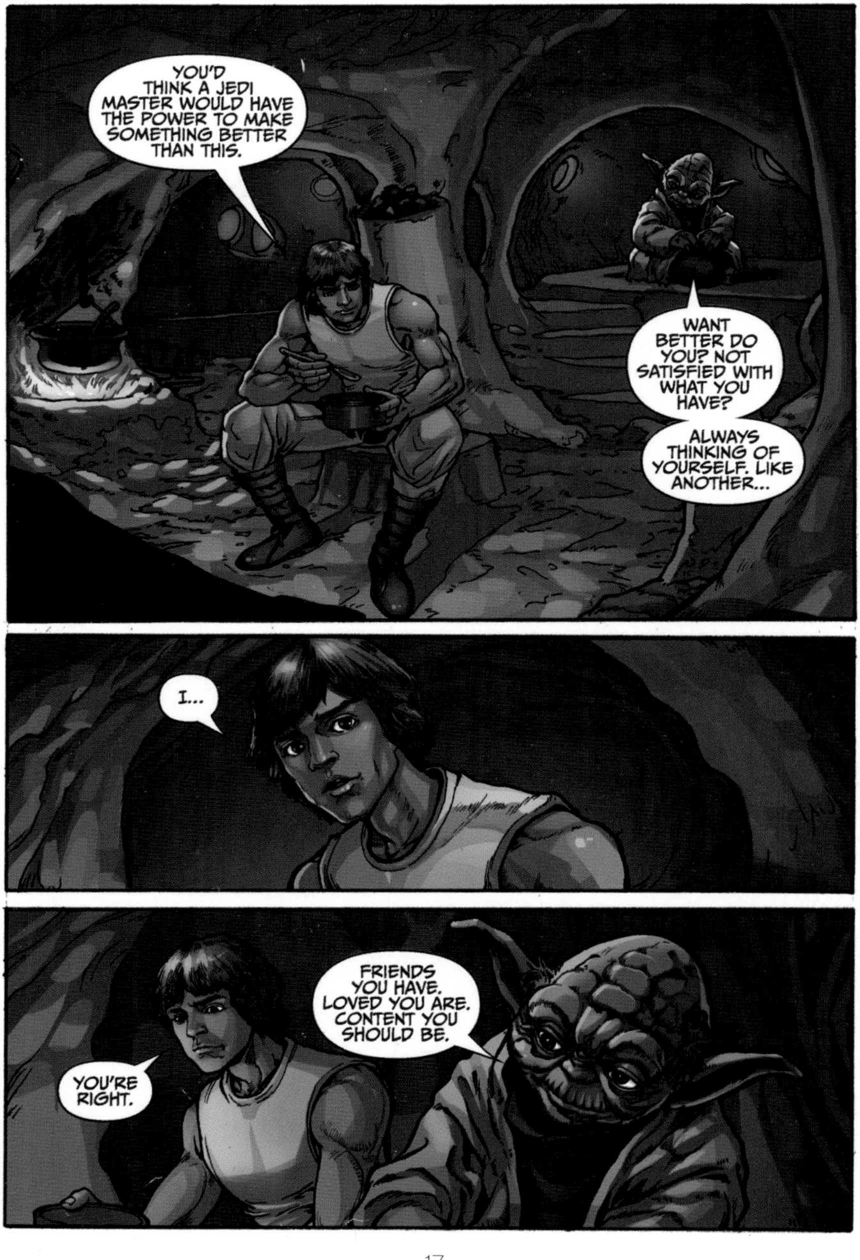
YOU'D THINK A JEDI MASTER WOULD HAVE THE POWER TO MAKE SOMETHING BETTER THAN THIS.
WANT BETTER DO YOU? NOT SATISFIED WITH WHAT YOU HAVE?
ALWAYS THINKING OF YOURSELF. LIKE ANOTHER...
I...
FRIENDS YOU HAVE. LOVED YOU ARE. CONTENT YOU SHOULD BE.
YOU'RE RIGHT.

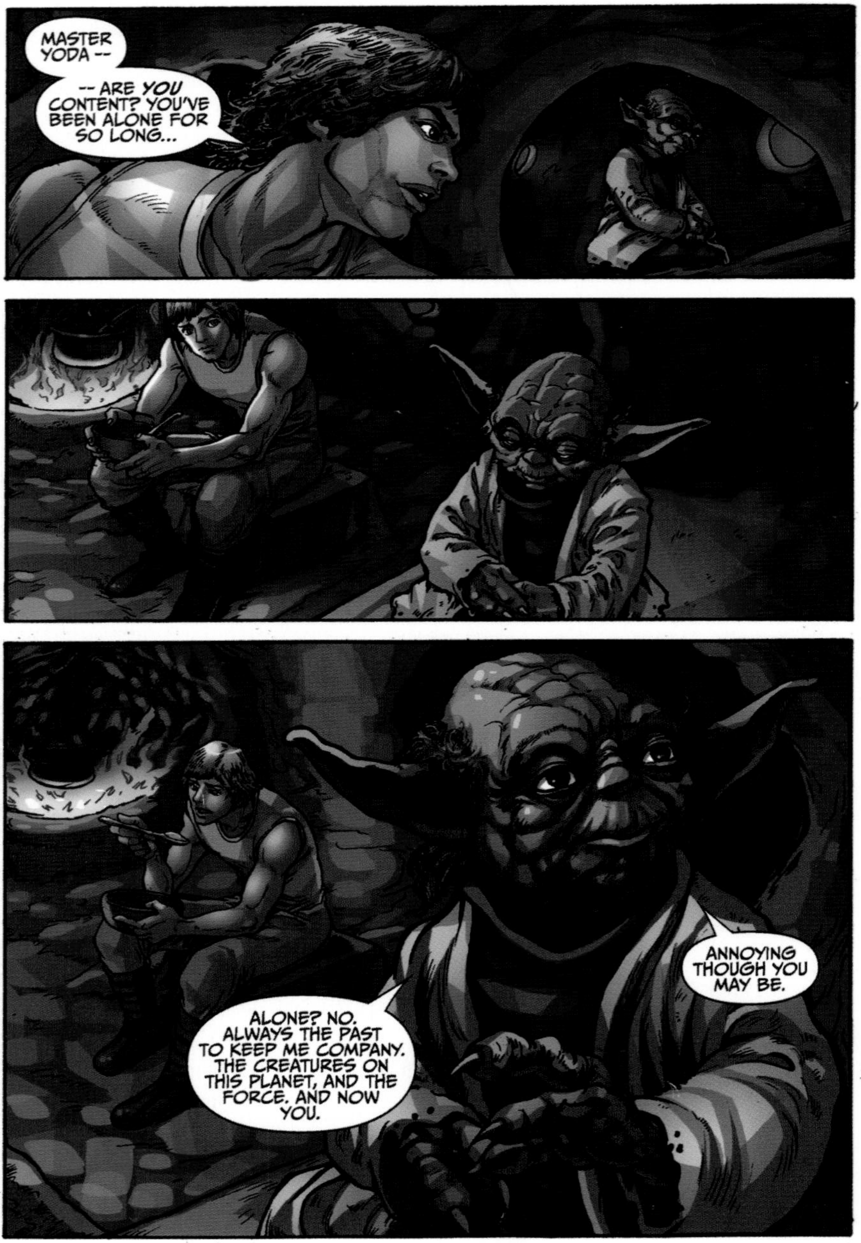
MASTER YODA --
-- ARE *YOU* CONTENT? YOU'VE BEEN ALONE FOR SO LONG...
ALONE? NO. ALWAYS THE PAST TO KEEP ME COMPANY. THE CREATURES ON THIS PLANET, AND THE FORCE. AND NOW YOU.
ANNOYING THOUGH YOU MAY BE.

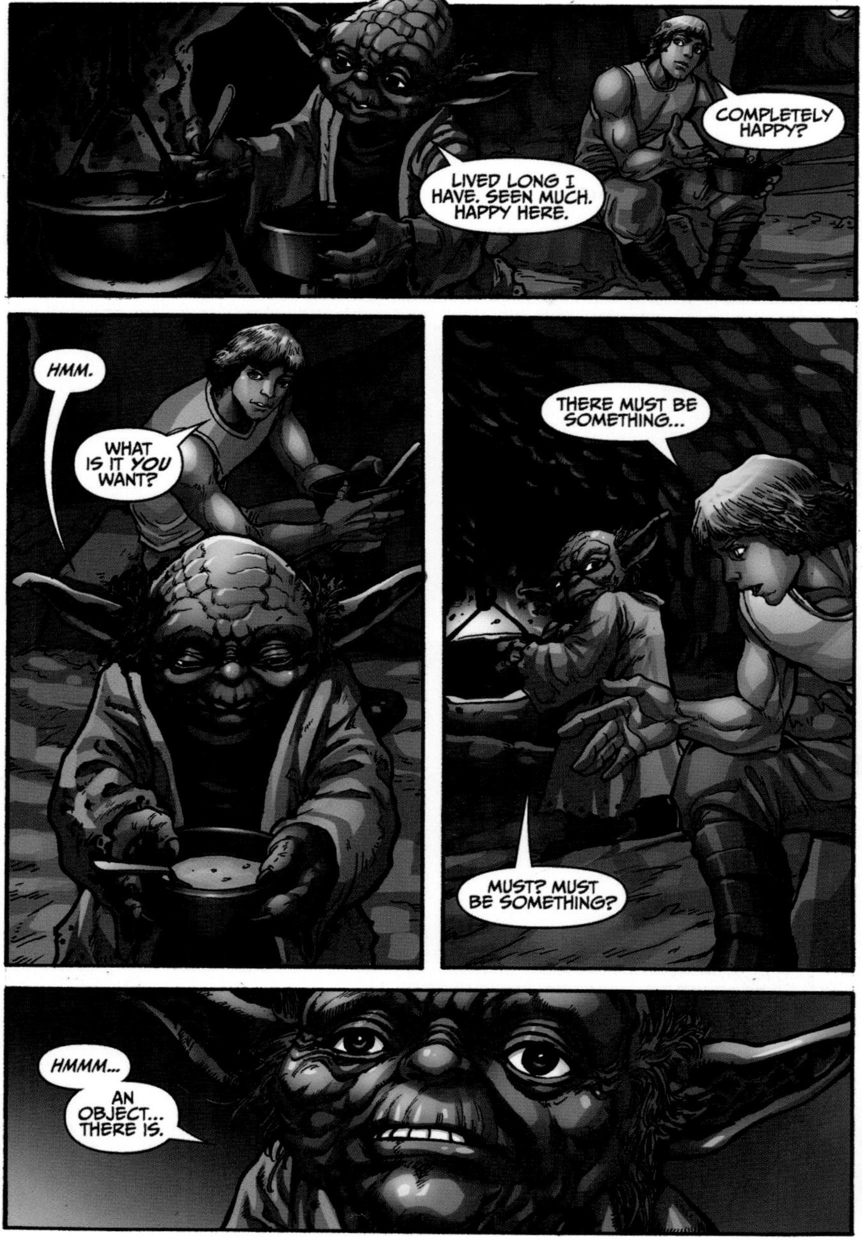
COMPLETELY HAPPY?
LIVED LONG I HAVE. SEEN MUCH. HAPPY HERE.
HMM.
WHAT IS IT YOU WANT?
THERE MUST BE SOMETHING...
MUST? MUST BE SOMETHING?
HMMM...
AN OBJECT... THERE IS.

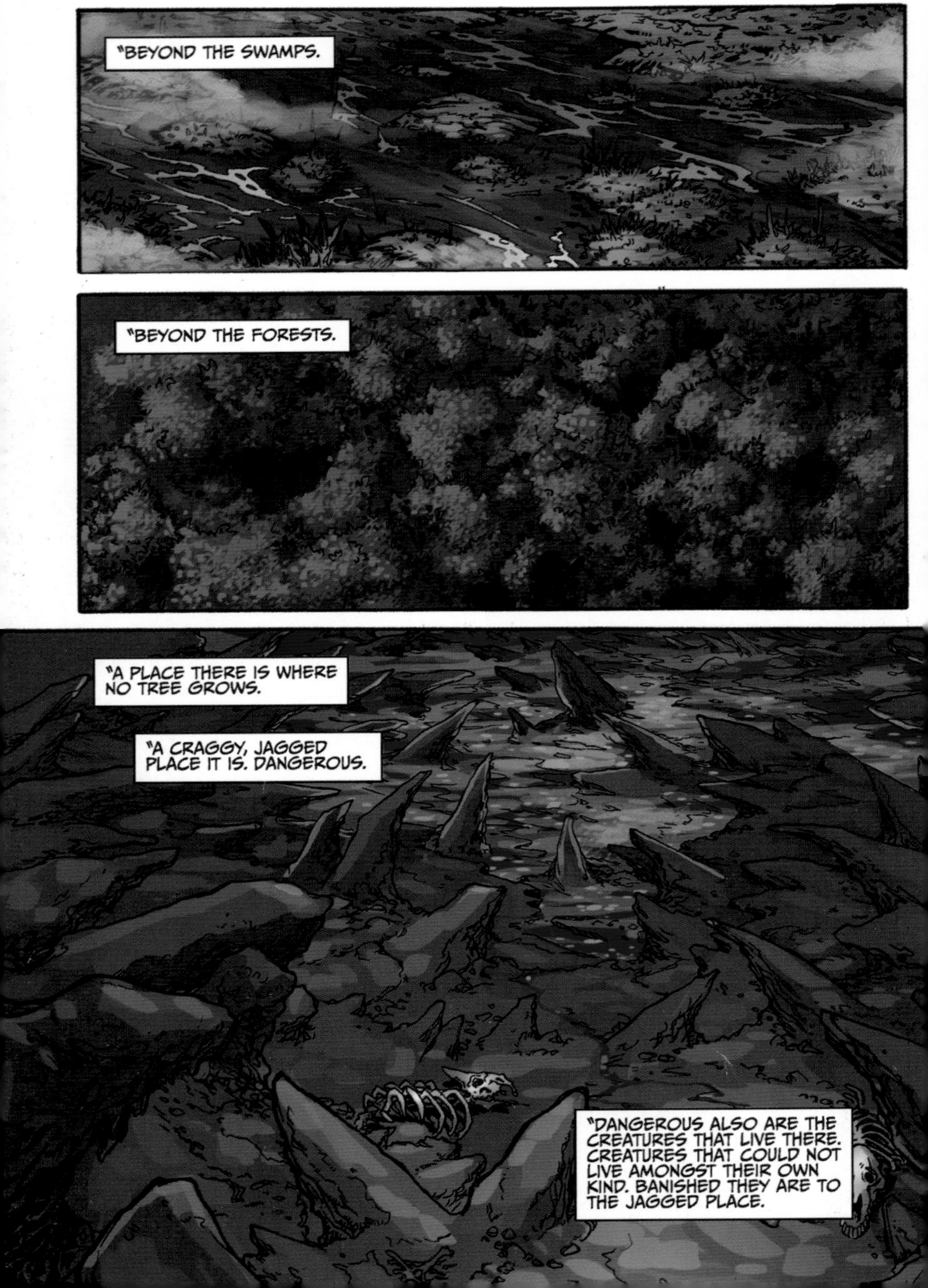
"BEYOND THE SWAMPS.
"BEYOND THE FORESTS.
"A PLACE THERE IS WHERE NO TREE GROWS.
"A CRAGGY, JAGGED PLACE IT IS. DANGEROUS.
"DANGEROUS ALSO ARE THE CREATURES THAT LIVE THERE. CREATURES THAT COULD NOT LIVE AMONGST THEIR OWN KIND. BANISHED THEY ARE TO THE JAGGED PLACE.

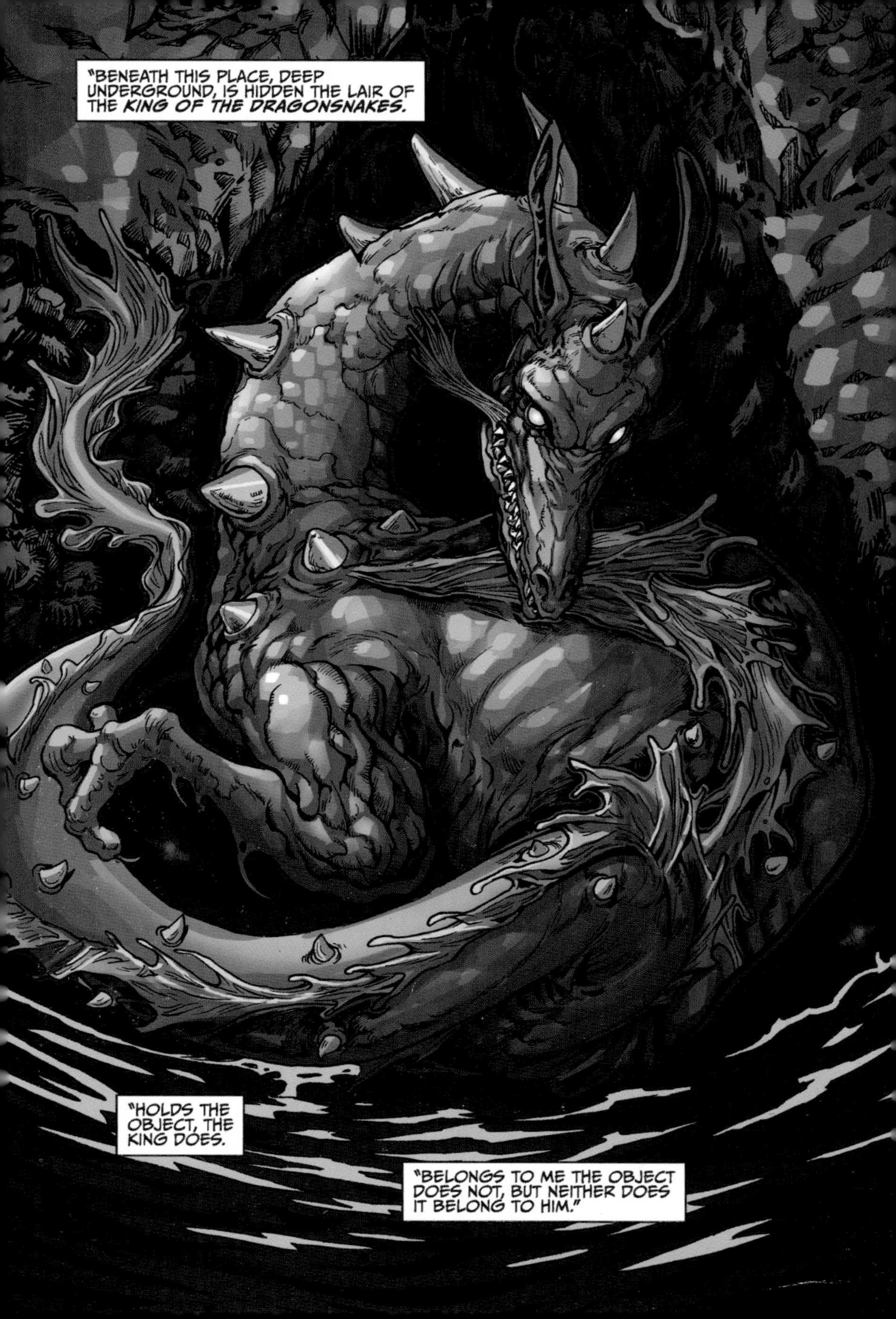
"BENEATH THIS PLACE, DEEP UNDERGROUND, IS HIDDEN THE LAIR OF THE *KING OF THE DRAGONSNAKES.*
"HOLDS THE OBJECT, THE KING DOES.
"BELONGS TO ME THE OBJECT DOES NOT, BUT NEITHER DOES IT BELONG TO HIM."

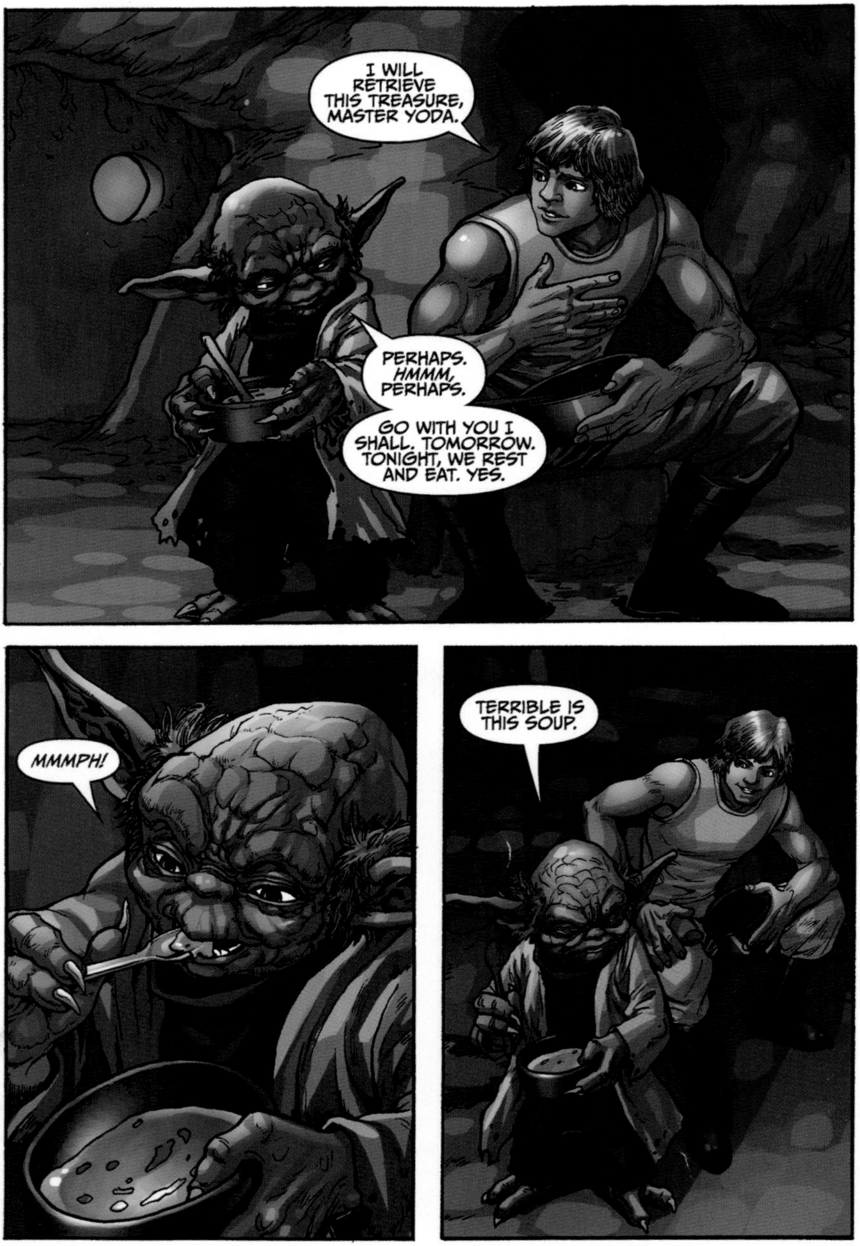
I WILL RETRIEVE THIS TREASURE, MASTER YODA.
PERHAPS. HMMM, PERHAPS.
GO WITH YOU I SHALL. TOMORROW. TONIGHT, WE REST AND EAT. YES.
MMMPH!
TERRIBLE IS THIS SOUP.

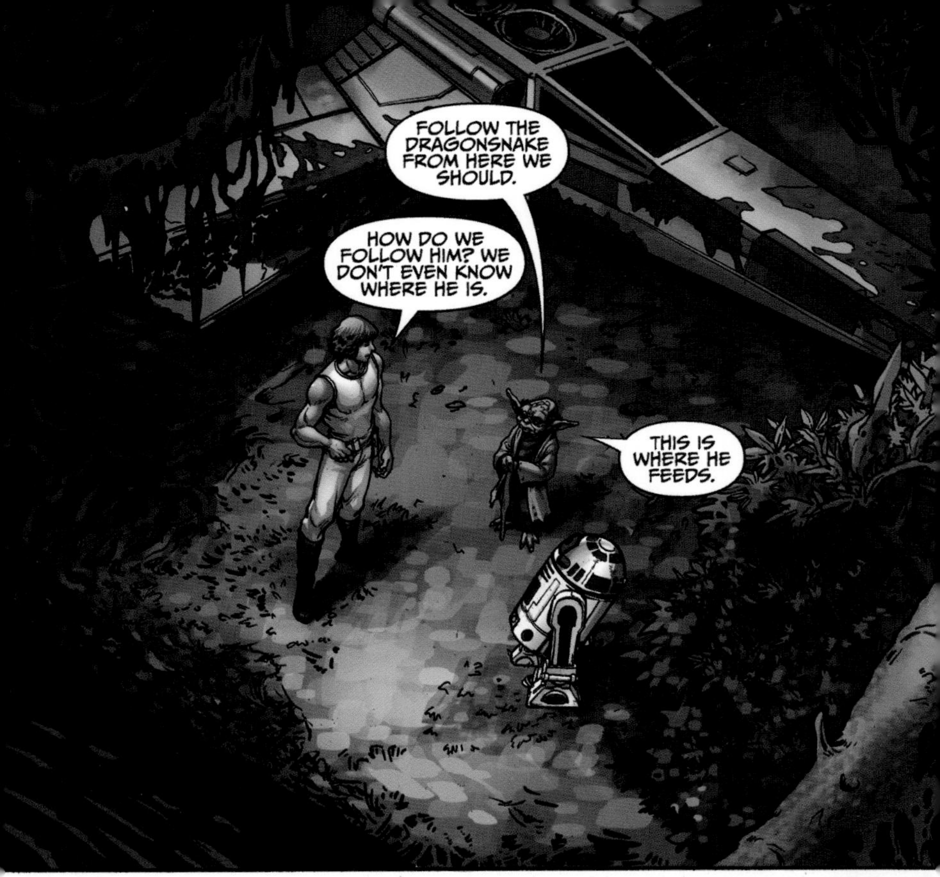
HOW DO WE FOLLOW HIM? WE DON'T EVEN KNOW WHERE HE IS.
FOLLOW THE DRAGONSNAKE FROM HERE WE SHOULD.
THIS IS WHERE HE FEEDS.

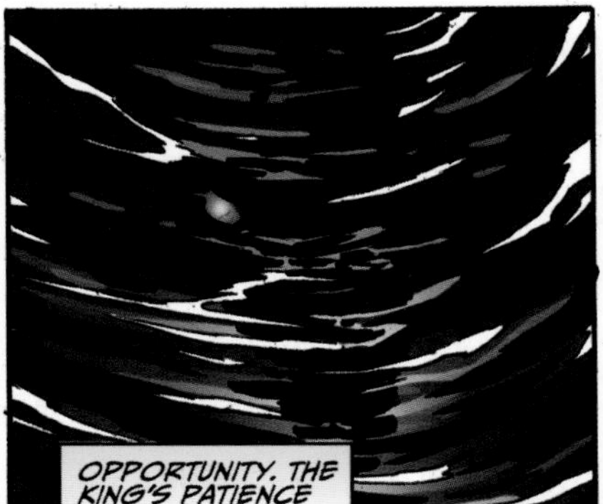
OPPORTUNITY. THE KING'S PATIENCE IS REWARDED.

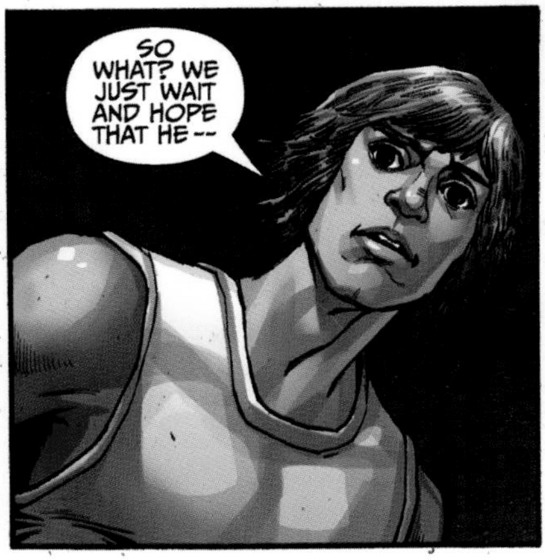
SO WHAT? WE JUST WAIT AND HOPE THAT HE--

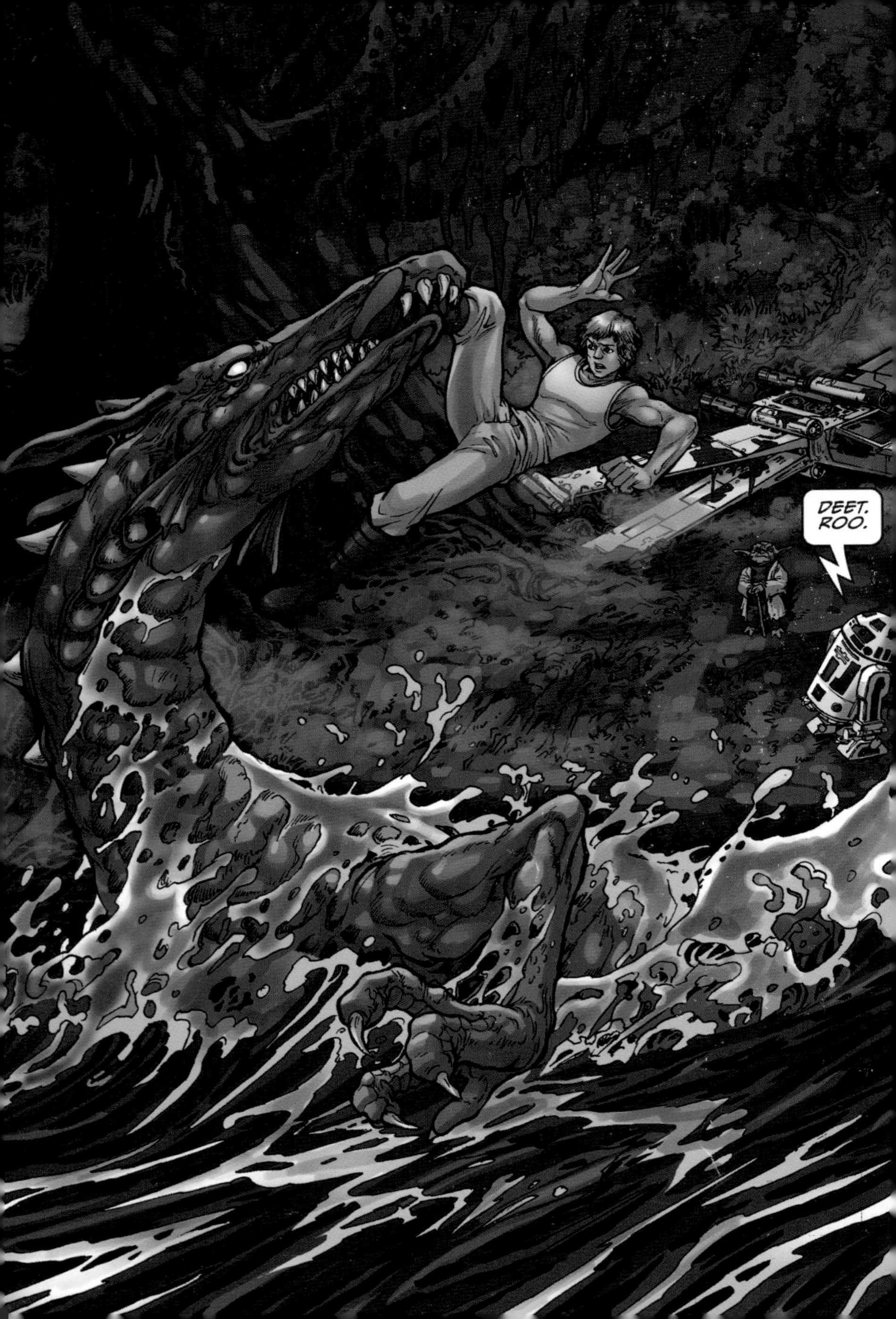
DEET. ROO.

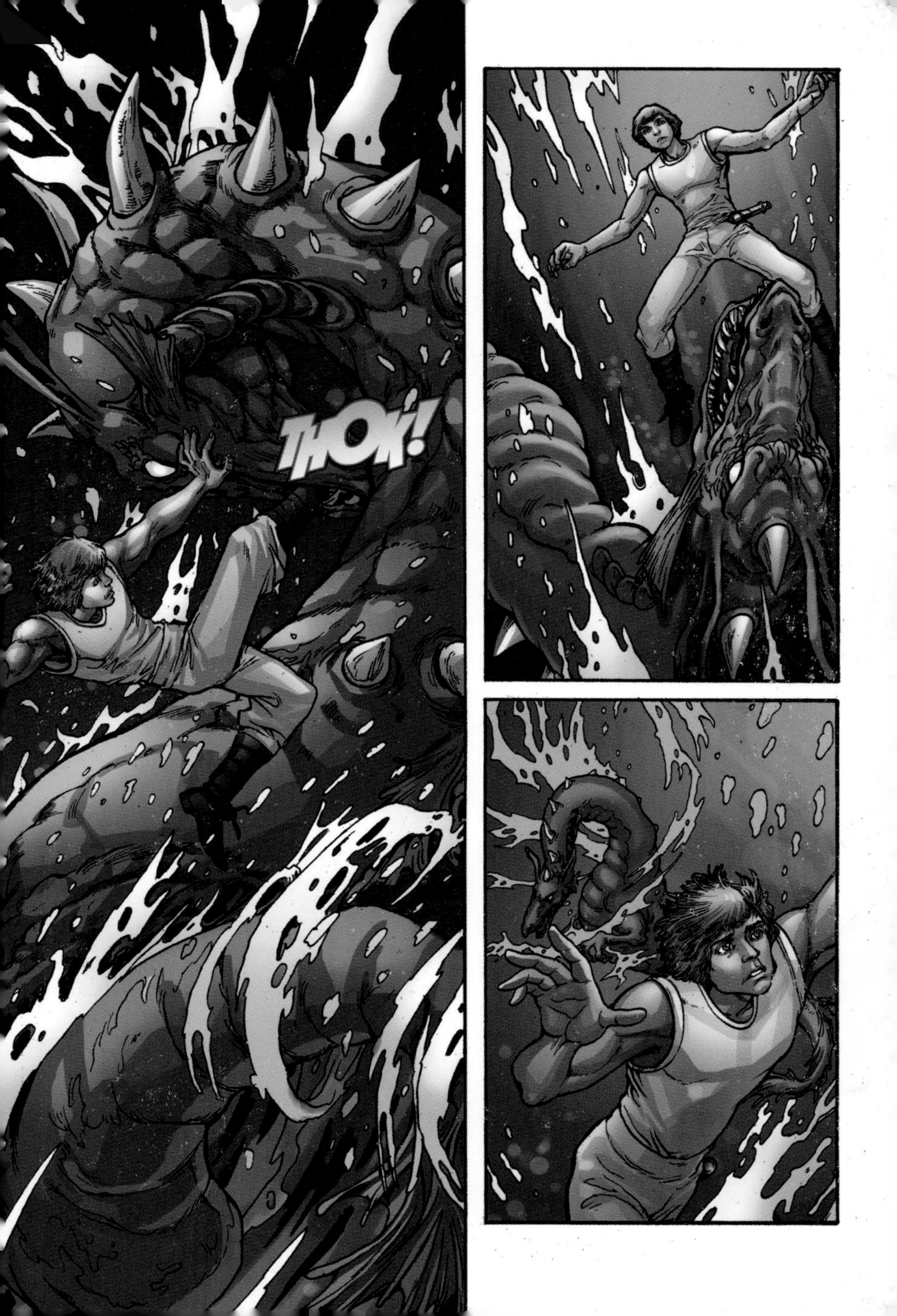
THOK!

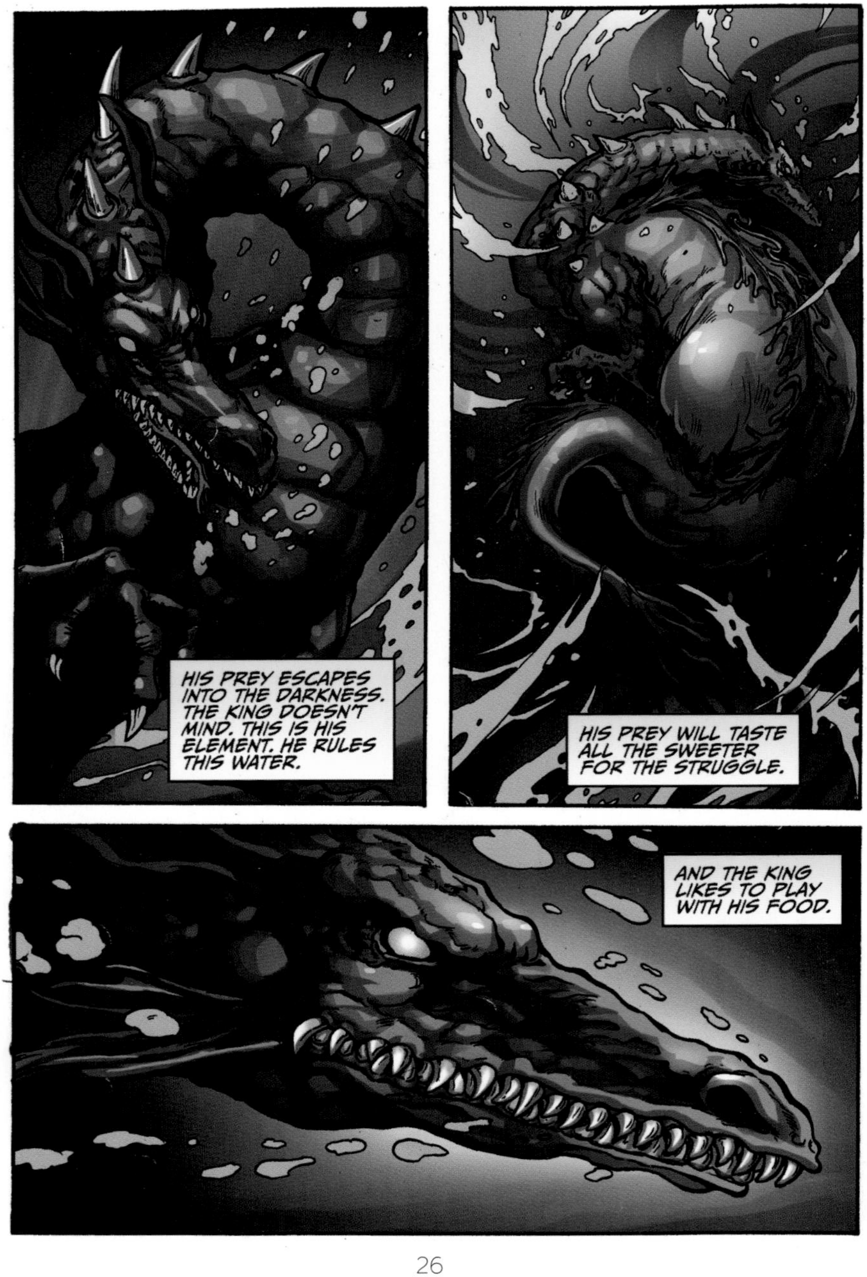
HIS PREY ESCAPES INTO THE DARKNESS. THE KING DOESN'T MIND. THIS IS HIS ELEMENT. HE RULES THIS WATER.
HIS PREY WILL TASTE ALL THE SWEETER FOR THE STRUGGLE.
AND THE KING LIKES TO PLAY WITH HIS FOOD.

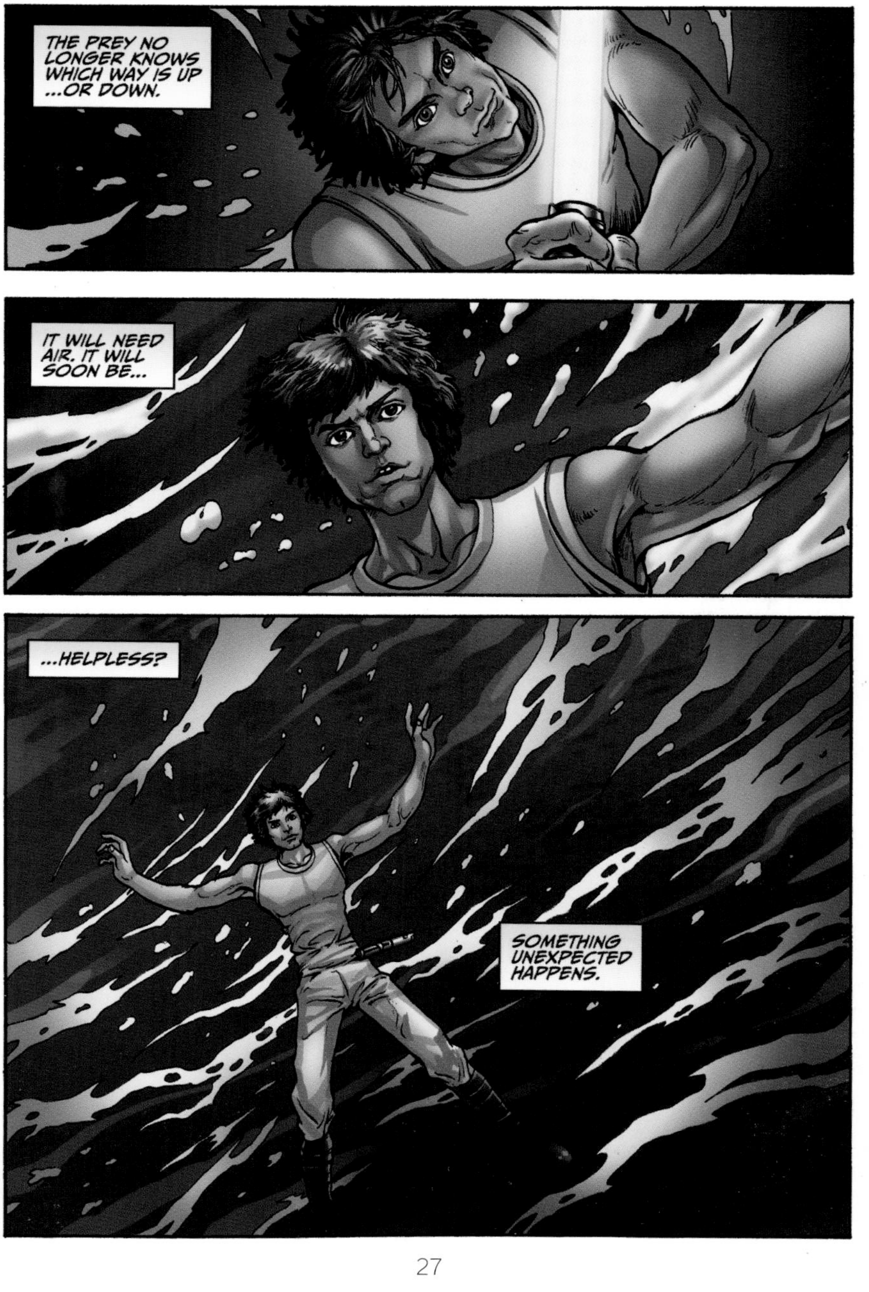
THE PREY NO LONGER KNOWS WHICH WAY IS UP ...OR DOWN.
IT WILL NEED AIR. IT WILL SOON BE...
...HELPLESS?
SOMETHING UNEXPECTED HAPPENS.

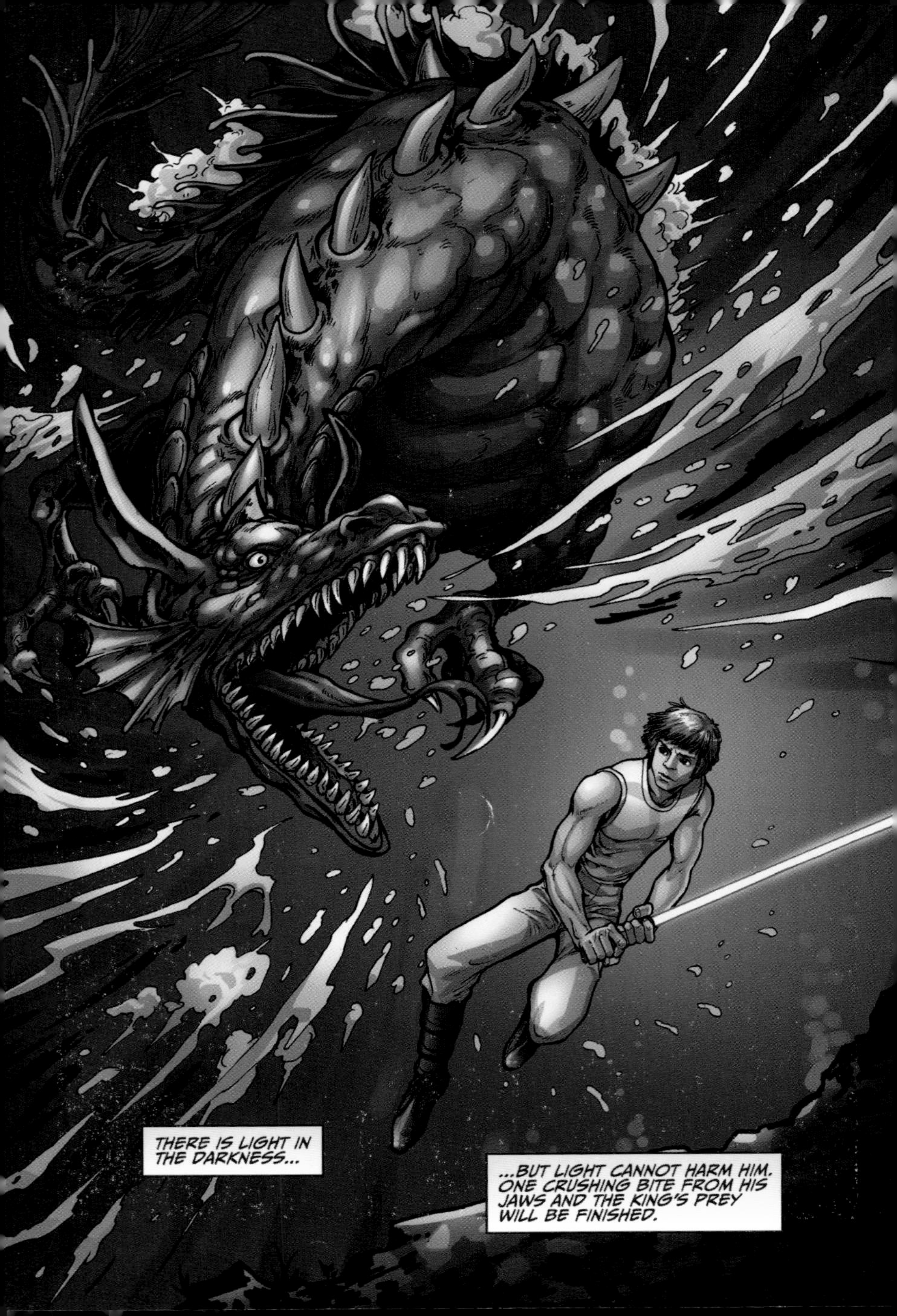
THERE IS LIGHT IN THE DARKNESS...
...BUT LIGHT CANNOT HARM HIM. ONE CRUSHING BITE FROM HIS JAWS AND THE KING'S PREY WILL BE FINISHED.

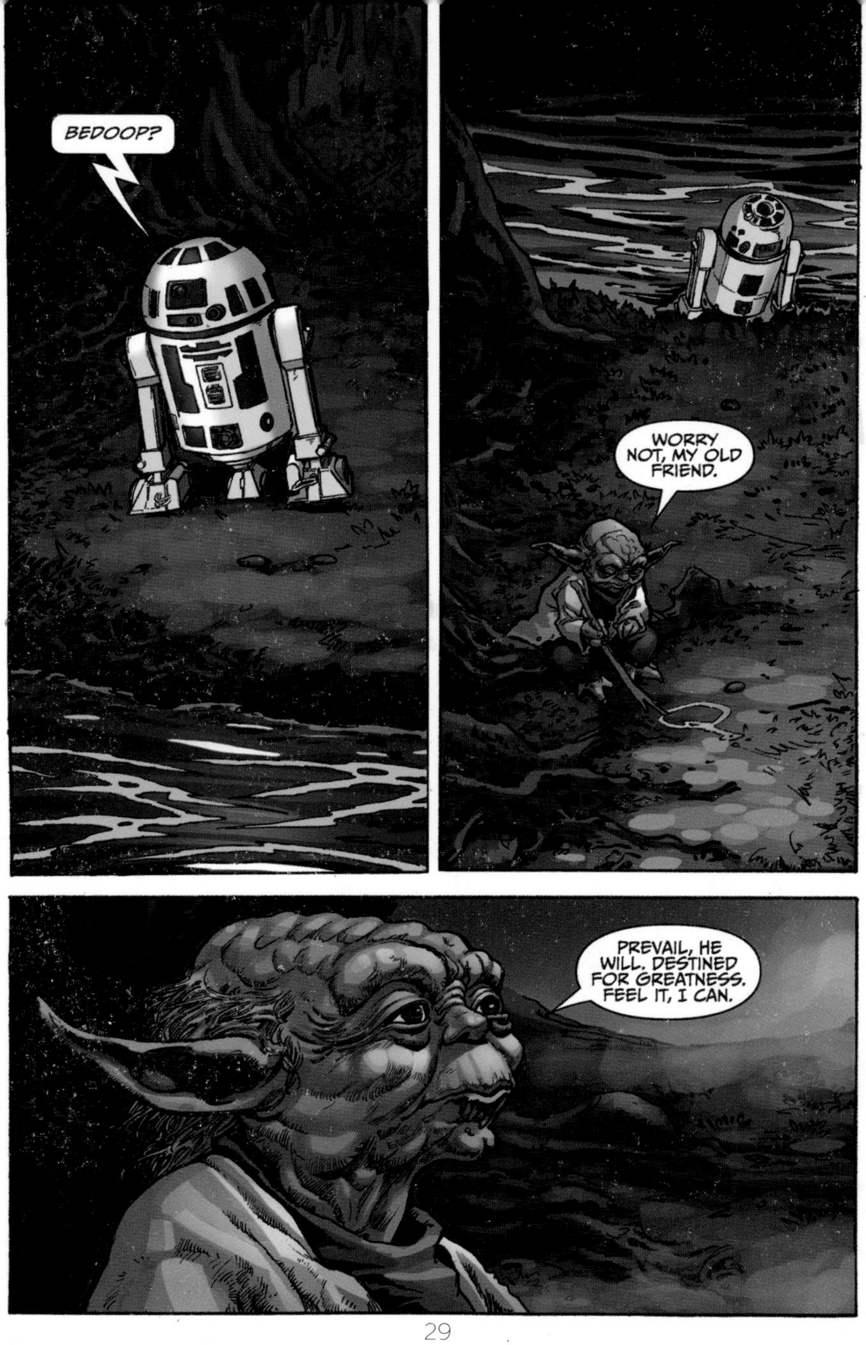
BEDOOP?
WORRY NOT, MY OLD FRIEND.
PREVAIL, HE WILL. DESTINED FOR GREATNESS. FEEL IT, I CAN.

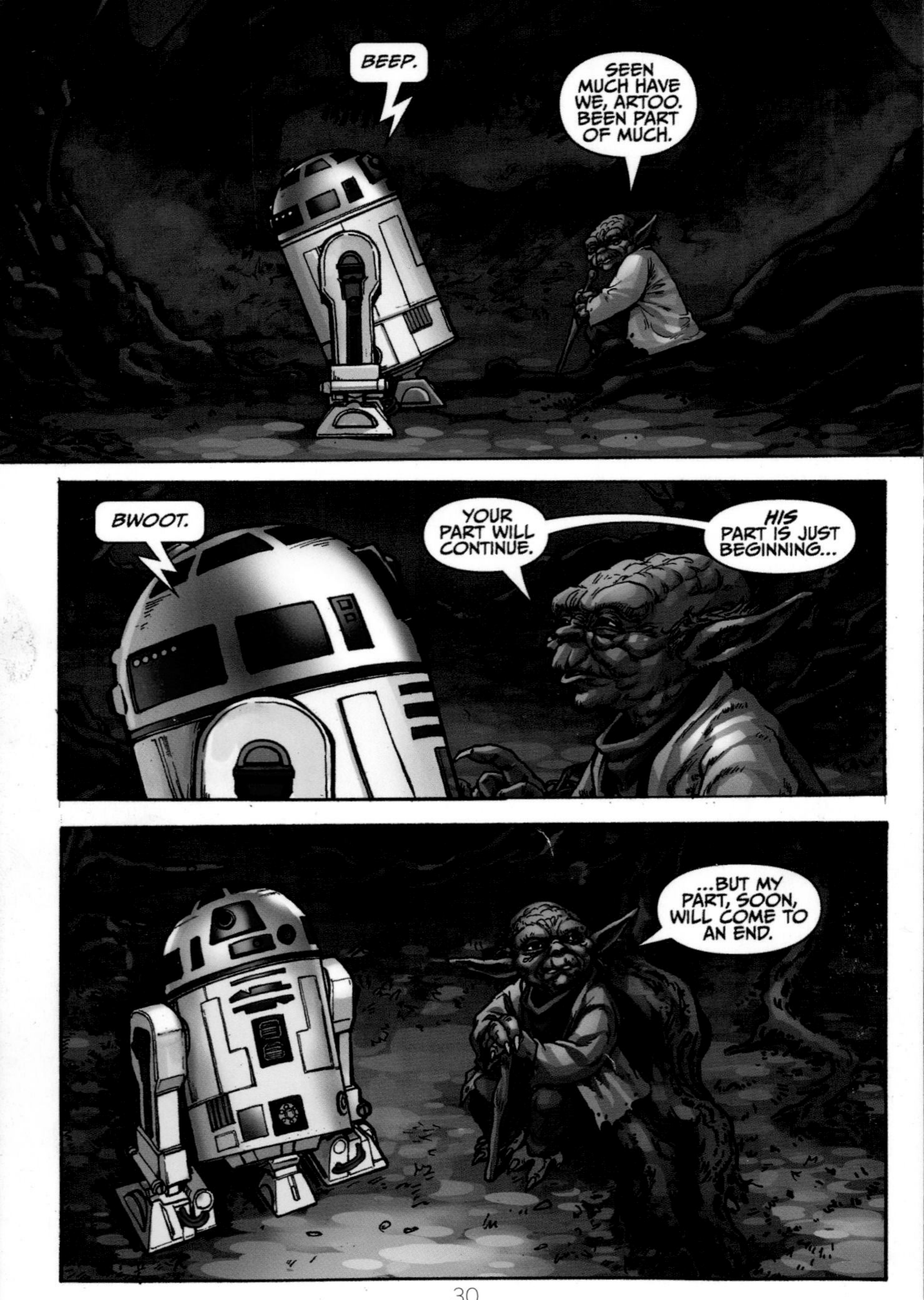
BEEP.
SEEN MUCH HAVE WE, ARTOO. BEEN PART OF MUCH.
BWOOT.
YOUR PART WILL CONTINUE.
HIS PART IS JUST BEGINNING...
...BUT MY PART, SOON, WILL COME TO AN END.

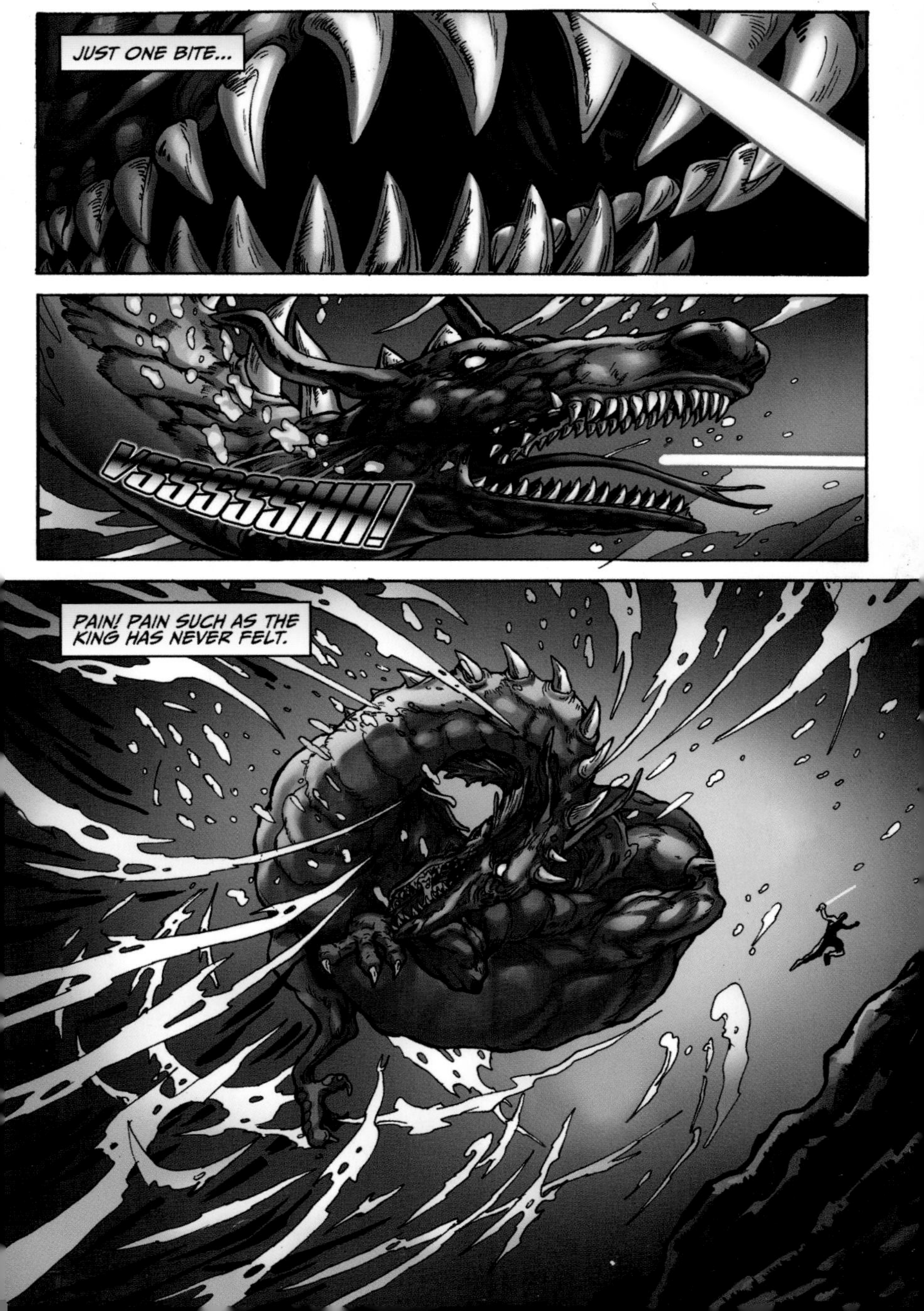
JUST ONE BITE...
VSSSSSSHH!
PAIN! PAIN SUCH AS THE KING HAS NEVER FELT.

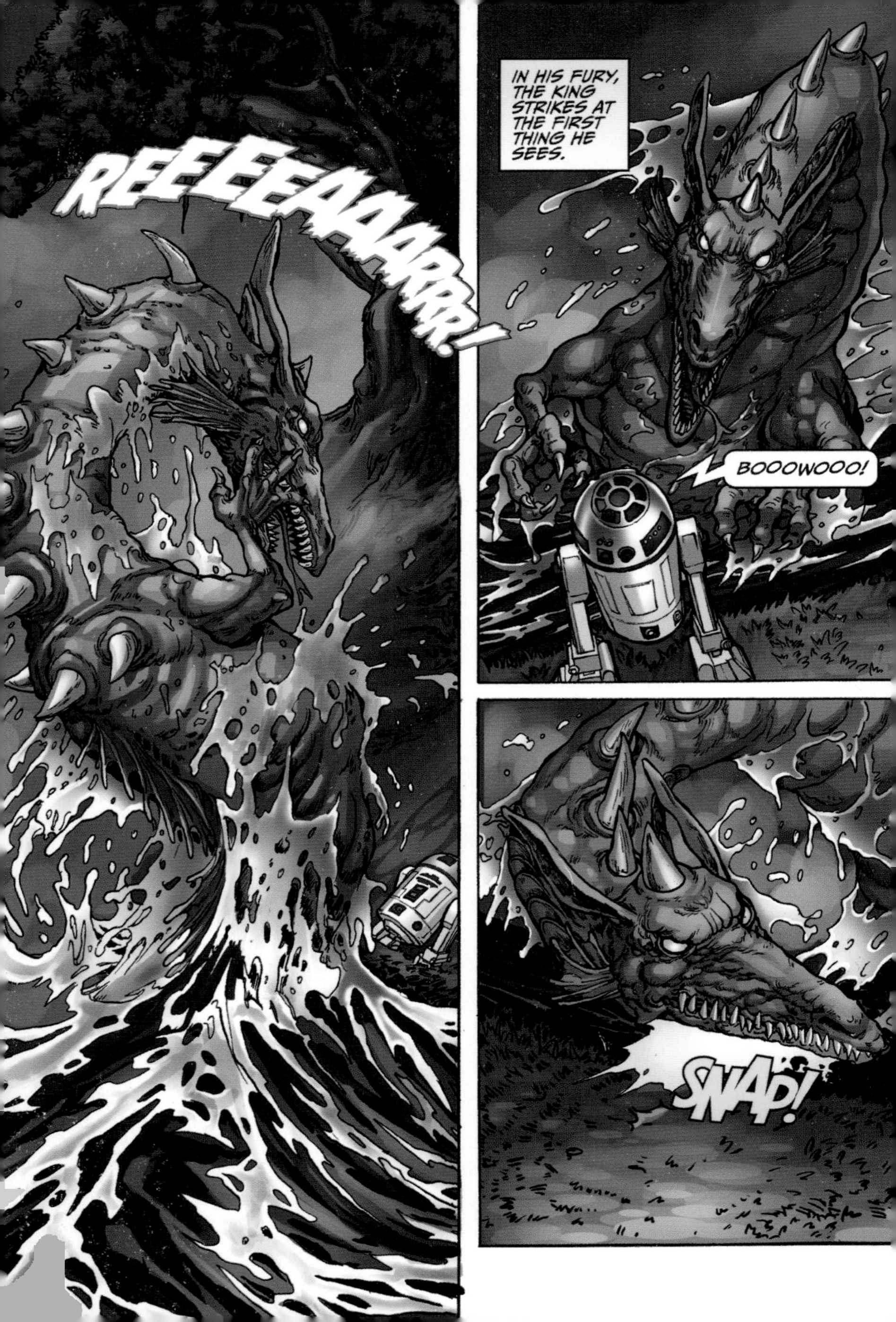
REEEEAAARRR!
IN HIS FURY, THE KING STRIKES AT THE FIRST THING HE SEES.
BOOOWOOO!
SNAP!

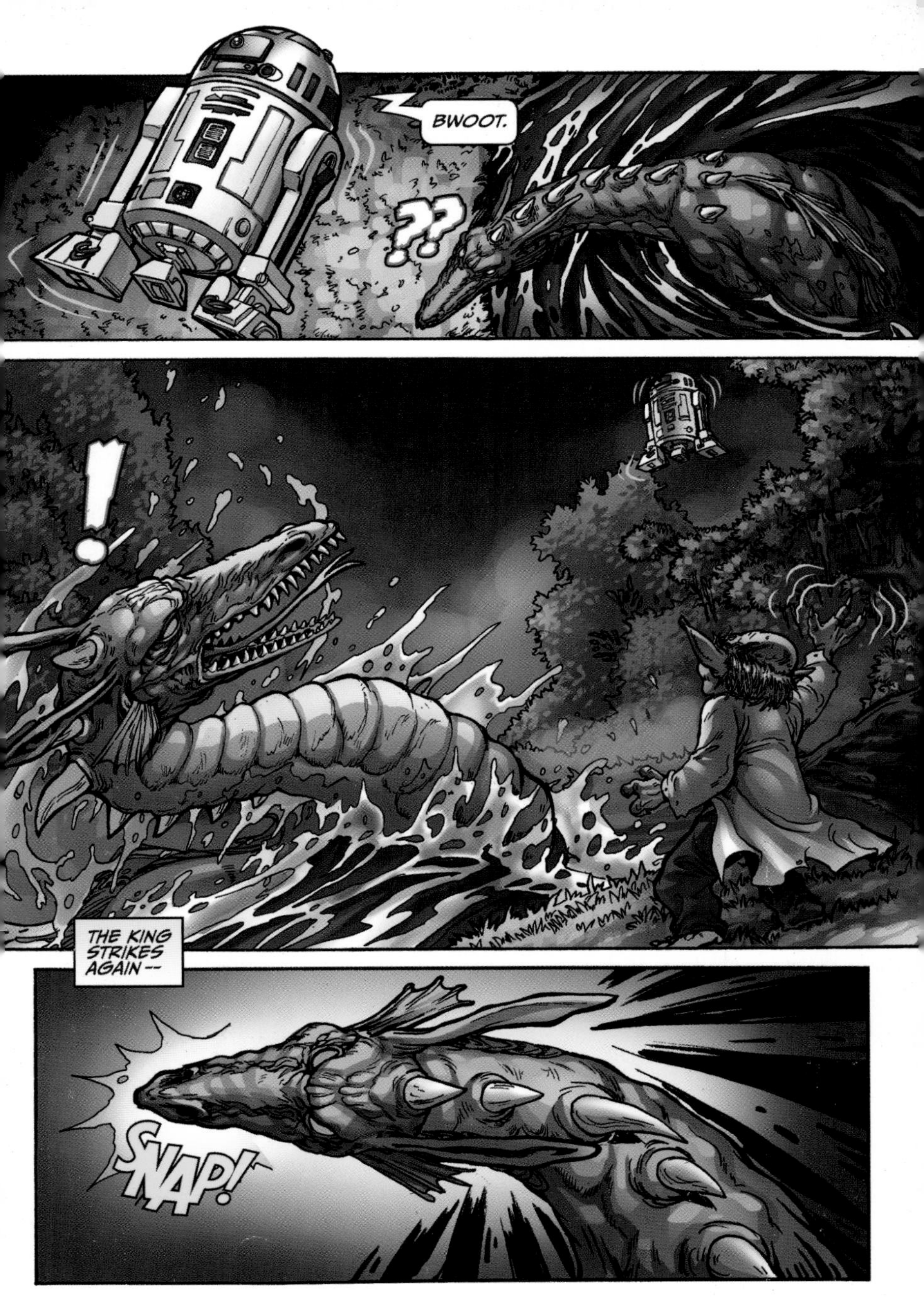
BWOOT.
??
!
THE KING STRIKES AGAIN --
SNAP!

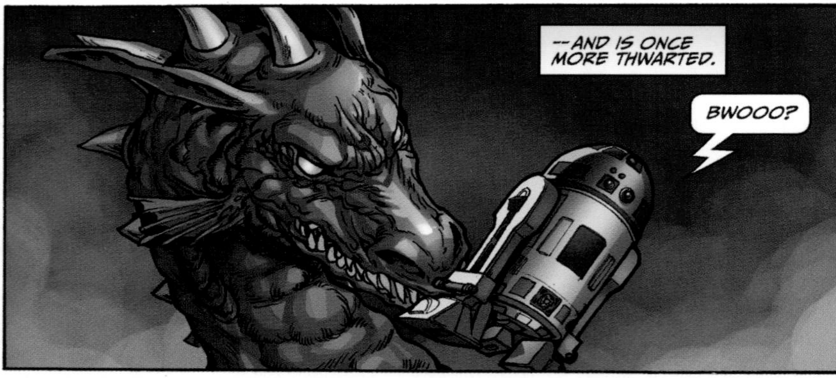
--AND IS ONCE MORE THWARTED.
BWOOO?

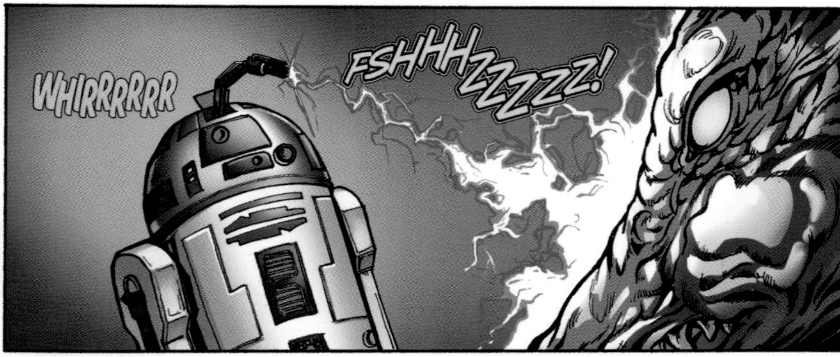
WHIRRRRRR
FSHHHZZZZZ!

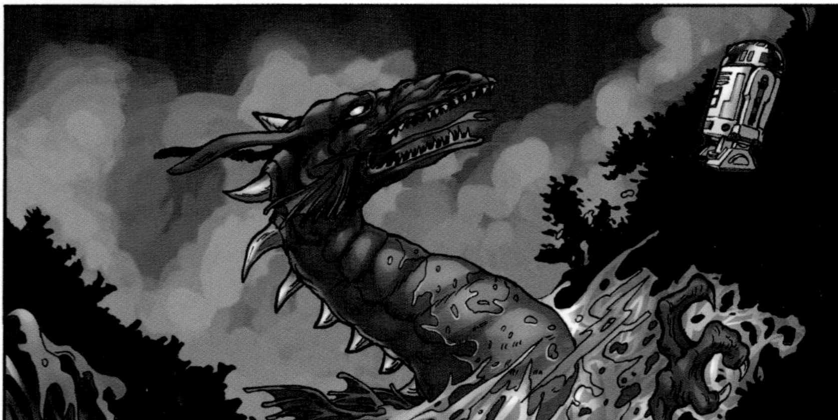

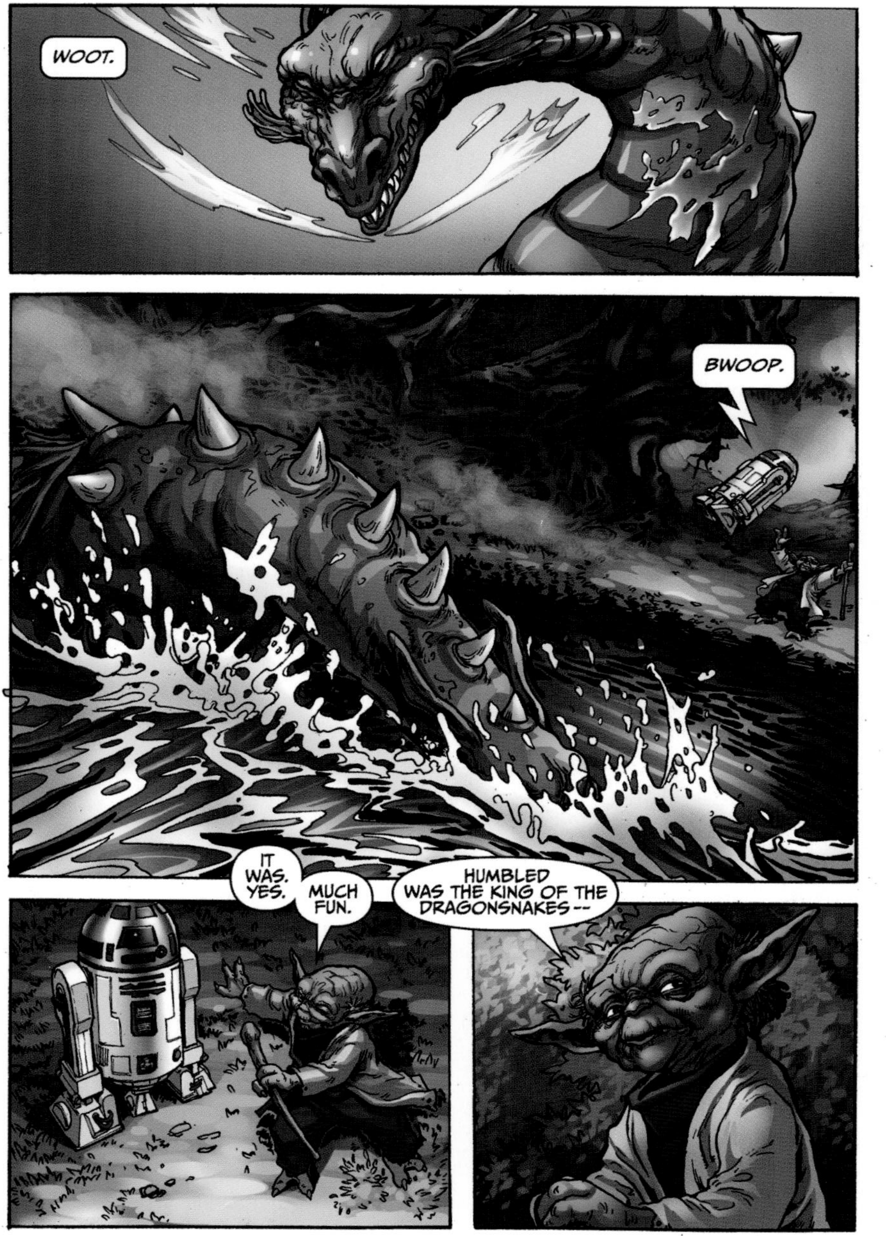
WOOT.
BWOOP.
IT WAS. YES.
MUCH FUN.
HUMBLED WAS THE KING OF THE DRAGONSNAKES --

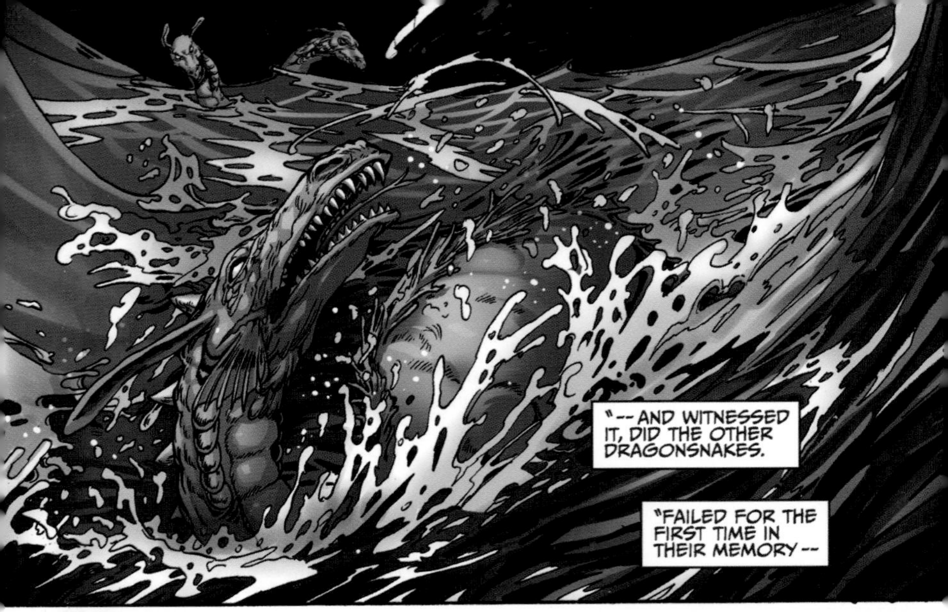
"-- AND WITNESSED IT, DID THE OTHER DRAGONSNAKES.
"FAILED FOR THE FIRST TIME IN THEIR MEMORY --

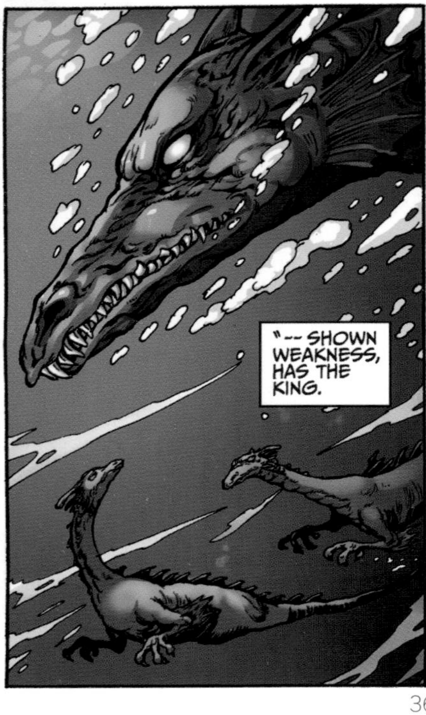
"-- SHOWN WEAKNESS, HAS THE KING.

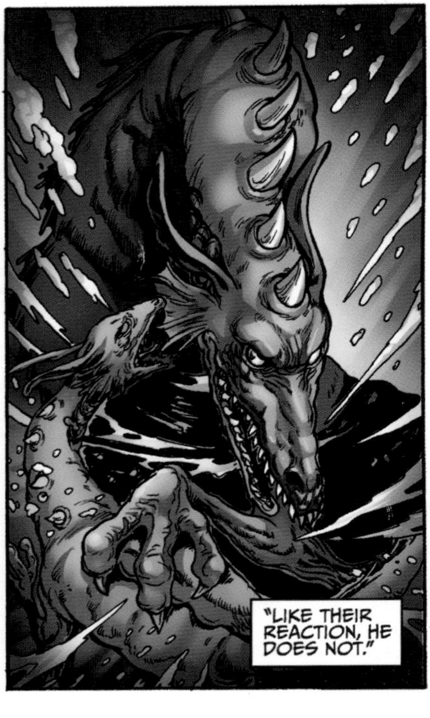
"LIKE THEIR REACTION, HE DOES NOT."

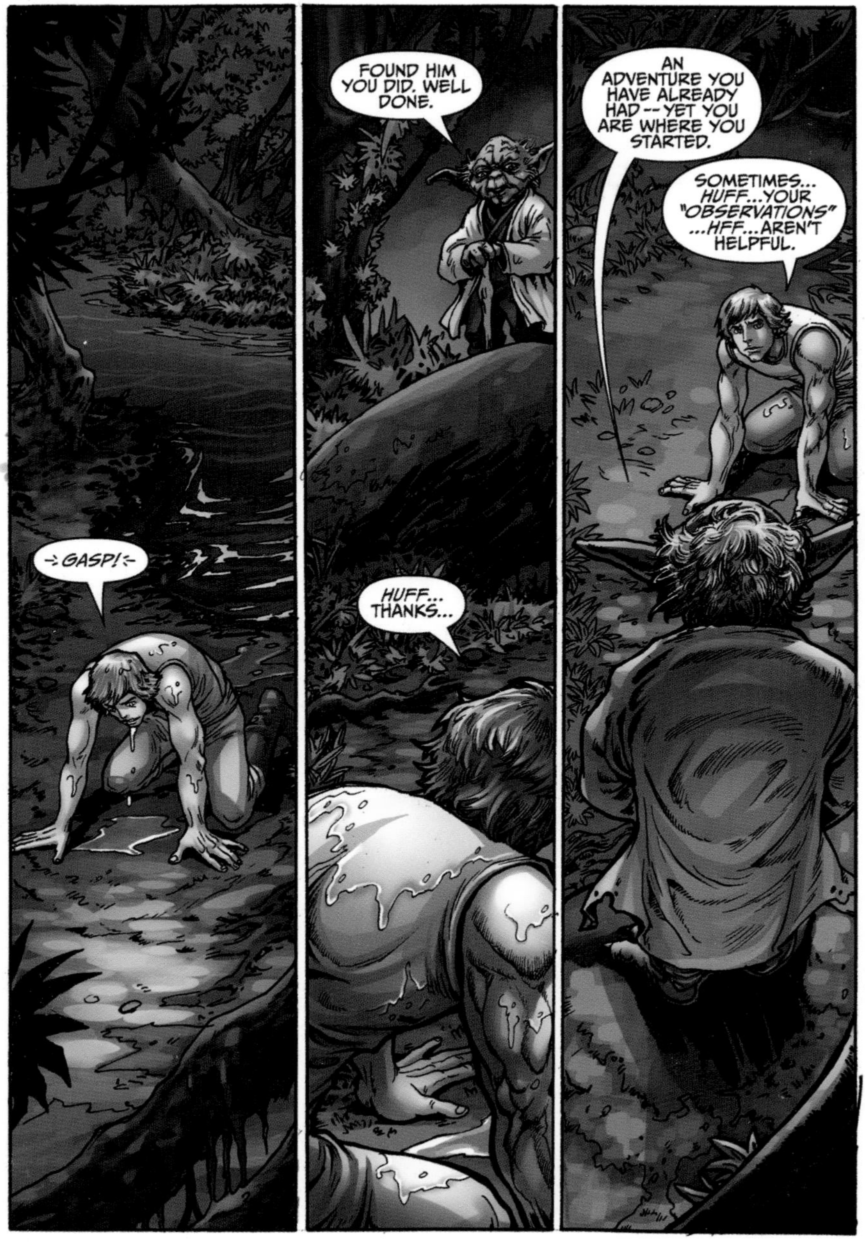
-GASP!-
FOUND HIM YOU DID. WELL DONE.
HUFF... THANKS...
AN ADVENTURE YOU HAVE ALREADY HAD--YET YOU ARE WHERE YOU STARTED.
SOMETIMES... HUFF...YOUR "OBSERVATIONS" ...HFF...AREN'T HELPFUL.

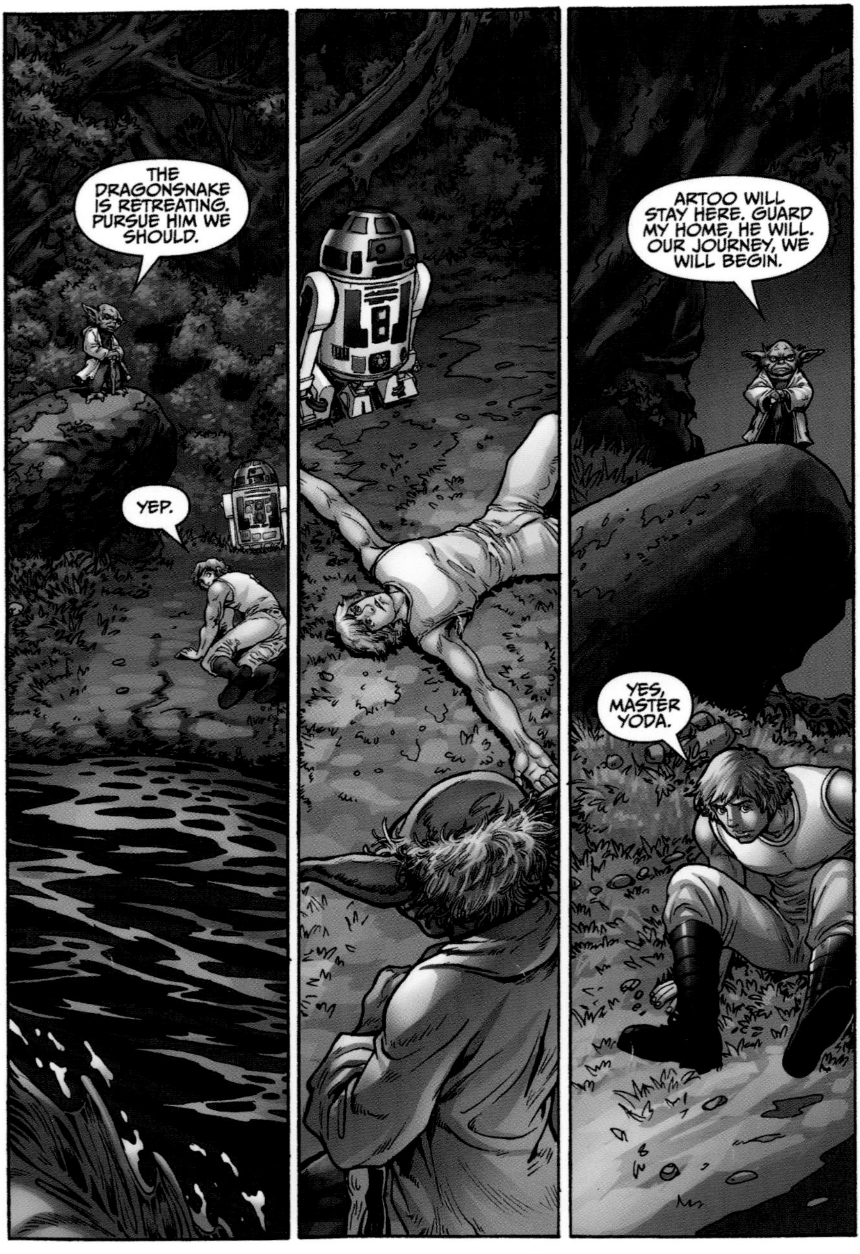
THE DRAGONSNAKE IS RETREATING. PURSUE HIM WE SHOULD.
YEP.
ARTOO WILL STAY HERE. GUARD MY HOME, HE WILL. OUR JOURNEY, WE WILL BEGIN.
YES, MASTER YODA.

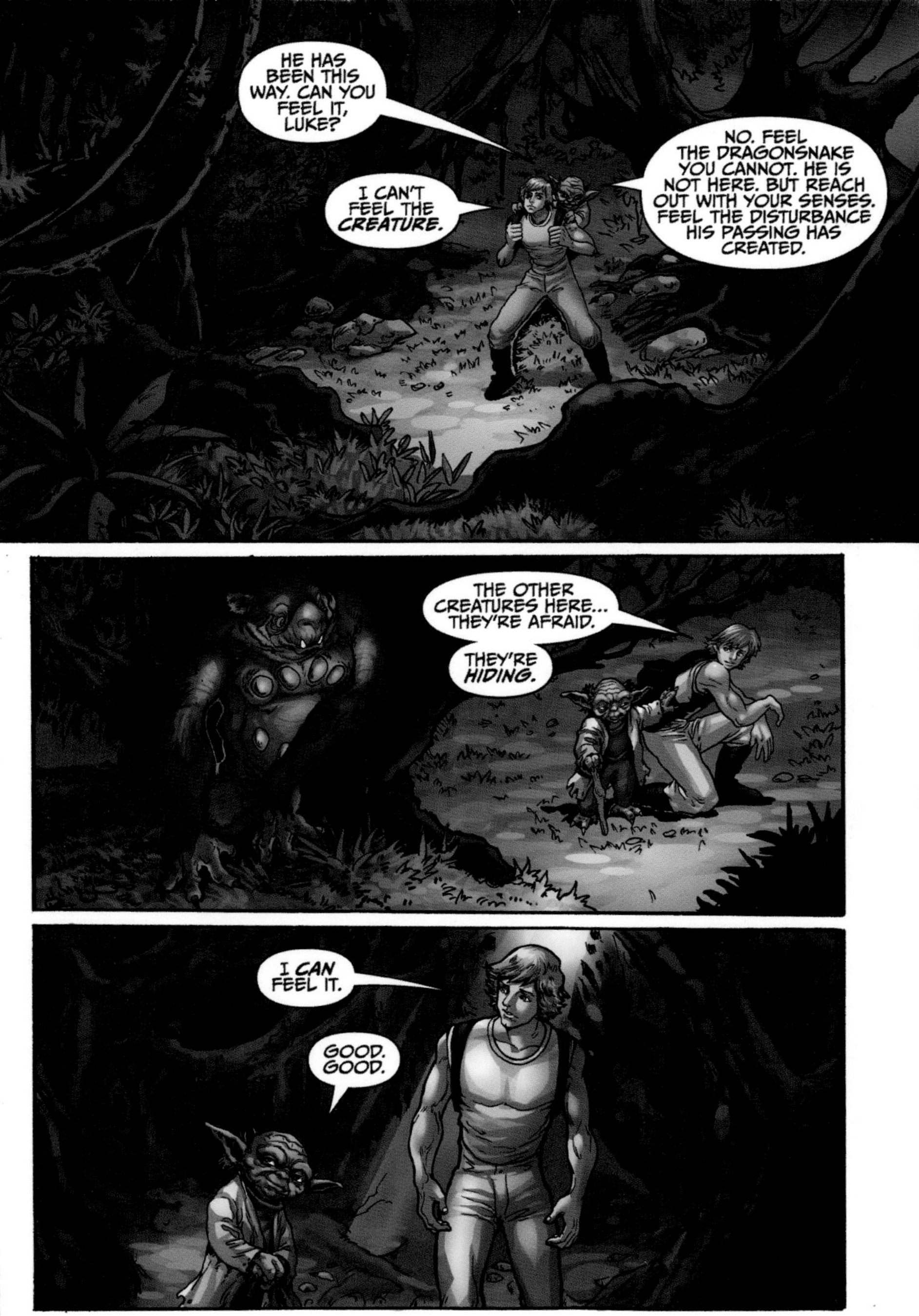
HE HAS BEEN THIS WAY. CAN YOU FEEL IT, LUKE?
I CAN'T FEEL THE *CREATURE.*
NO. FEEL THE DRAGONSNAKE YOU CANNOT. HE IS NOT HERE. BUT REACH OUT WITH YOUR SENSES. FEEL THE DISTURBANCE HIS PASSING HAS CREATED.
THE OTHER CREATURES HERE... THEY'RE AFRAID.
THEY'RE *HIDING.*
I *CAN* FEEL IT.
GOOD. GOOD.

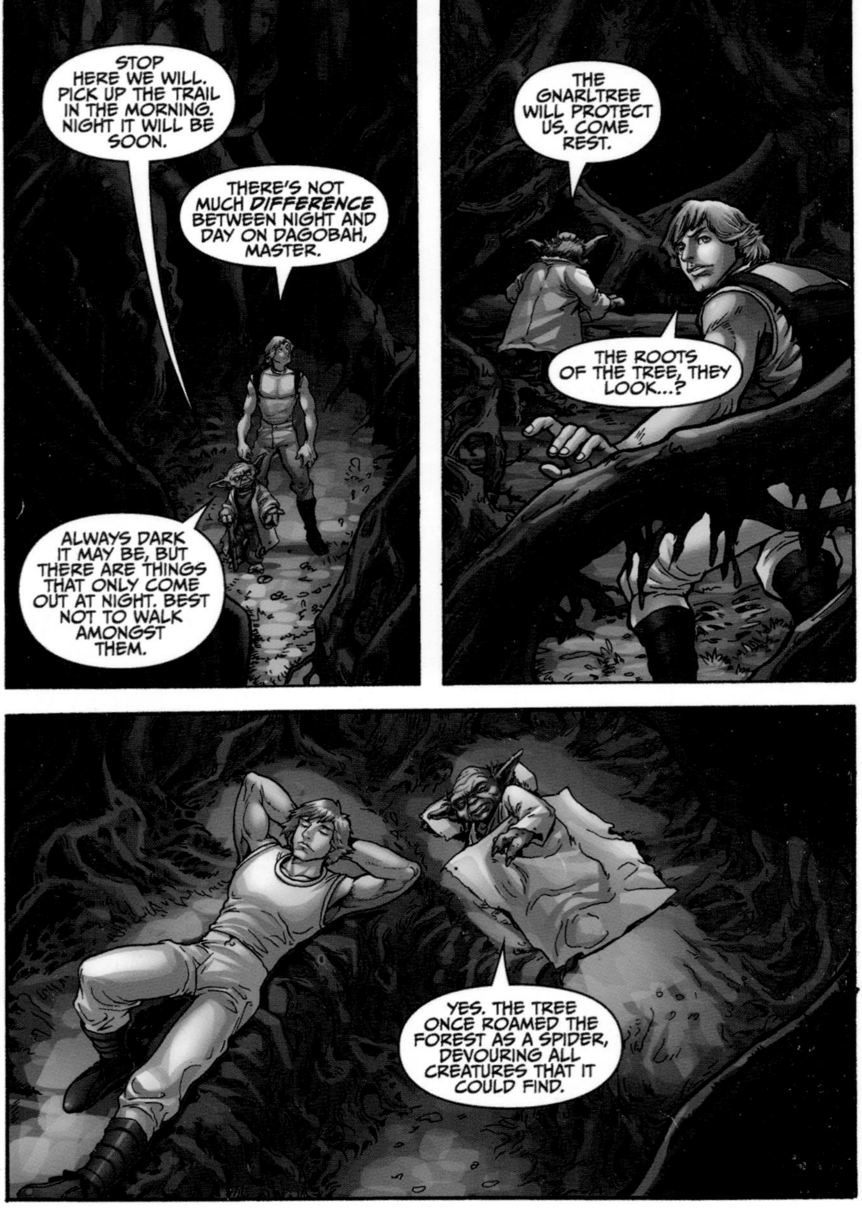
STOP HERE WE WILL. PICK UP THE TRAIL IN THE MORNING. NIGHT IT WILL BE SOON.
THERE'S NOT MUCH *DIFFERENCE* BETWEEN NIGHT AND DAY ON DAGOBAH, MASTER.
ALWAYS DARK IT MAY BE, BUT THERE ARE THINGS THAT ONLY COME OUT AT NIGHT. BEST NOT TO WALK AMONGST THEM.
THE GNARLTREE WILL PROTECT US. COME. REST.
THE ROOTS OF THE TREE, THEY LOOK...?
YES. THE TREE ONCE ROAMED THE FOREST AS A SPIDER, DEVOURING ALL CREATURES THAT IT COULD FIND.

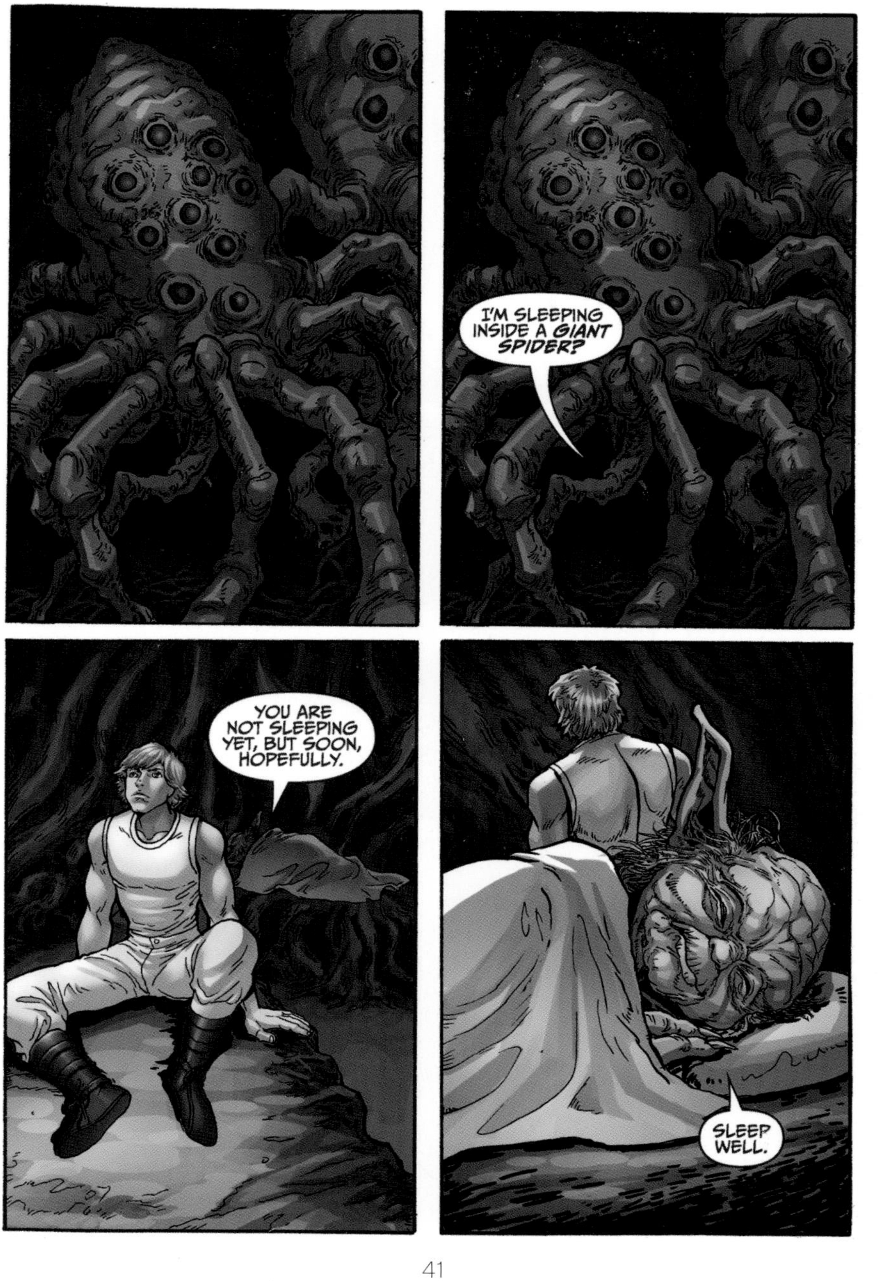
I'M SLEEPING INSIDE A GIANT SPIDER?
YOU ARE NOT SLEEPING YET, BUT SOON, HOPEFULLY.
SLEEP WELL.

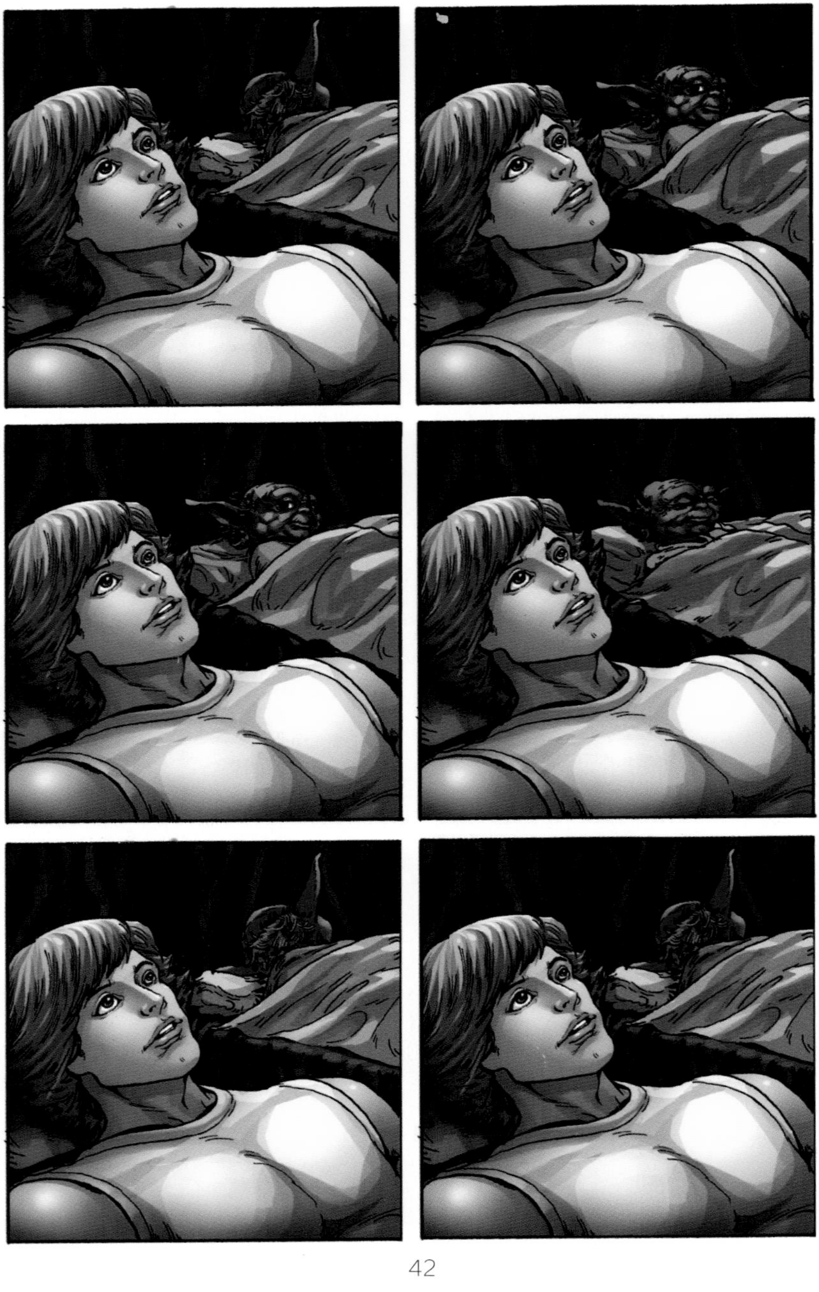

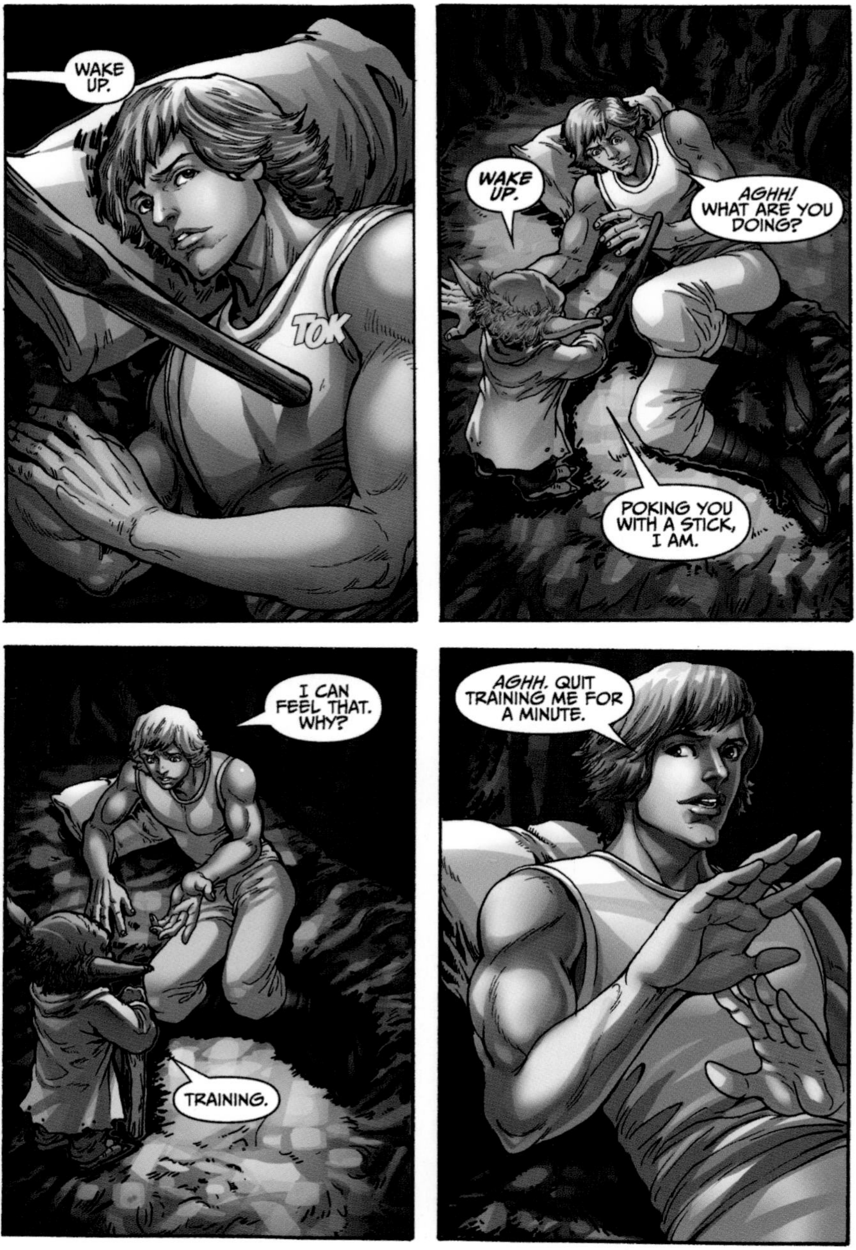
WAKE UP.
TOK
WAKE UP.
AGHH! WHAT ARE YOU DOING?
POKING YOU WITH A STICK, I AM.
I CAN FEEL THAT. WHY?
TRAINING.
AGHH. QUIT TRAINING ME FOR A MINUTE.

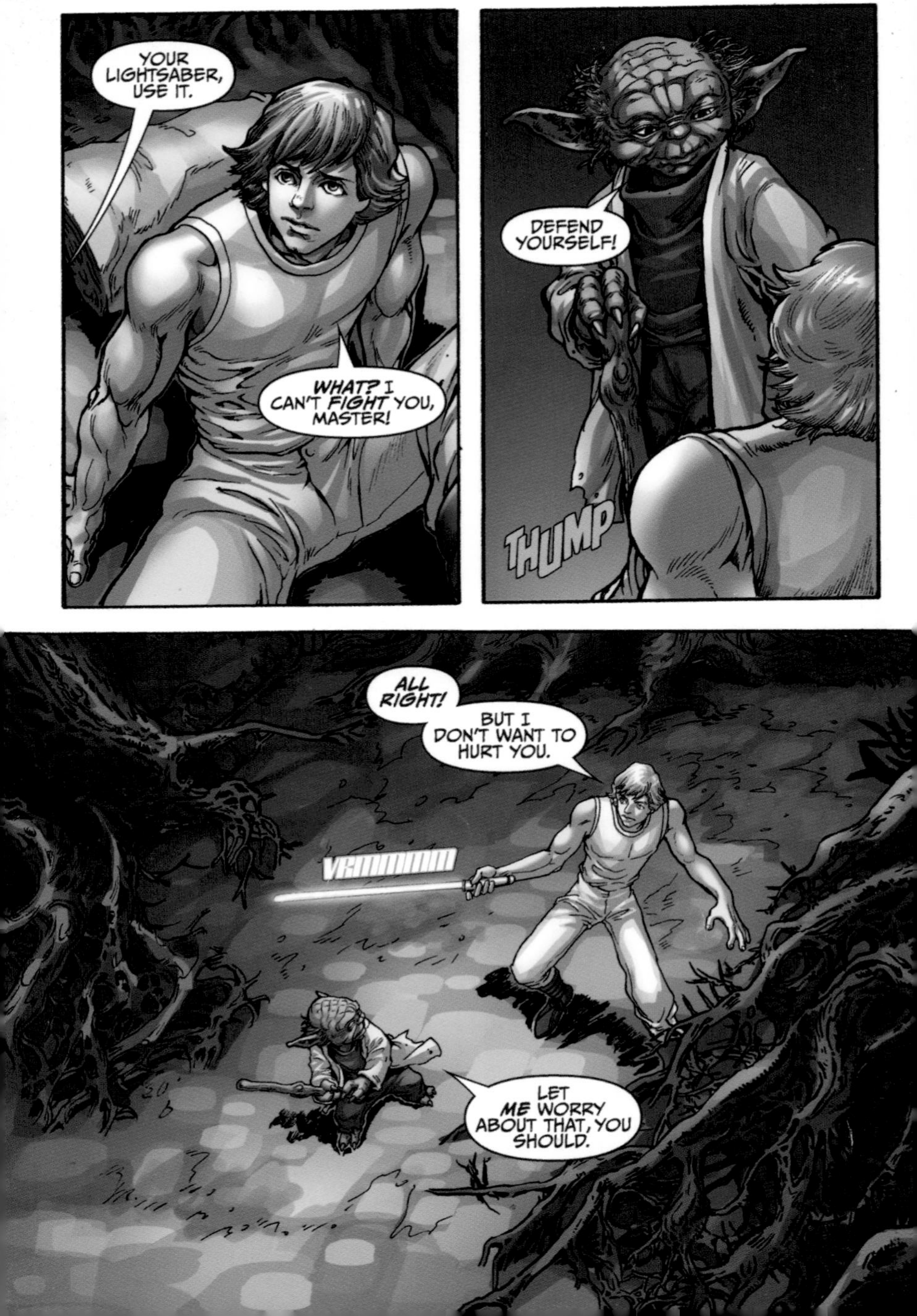
YOUR LIGHTSABER, USE IT.
WHAT? I CAN'T FIGHT YOU, MASTER!
DEFEND YOURSELF!
THUMP
ALL RIGHT!
BUT I DON'T WANT TO HURT YOU.
VRMMMM
LET ME WORRY ABOUT THAT, YOU SHOULD.

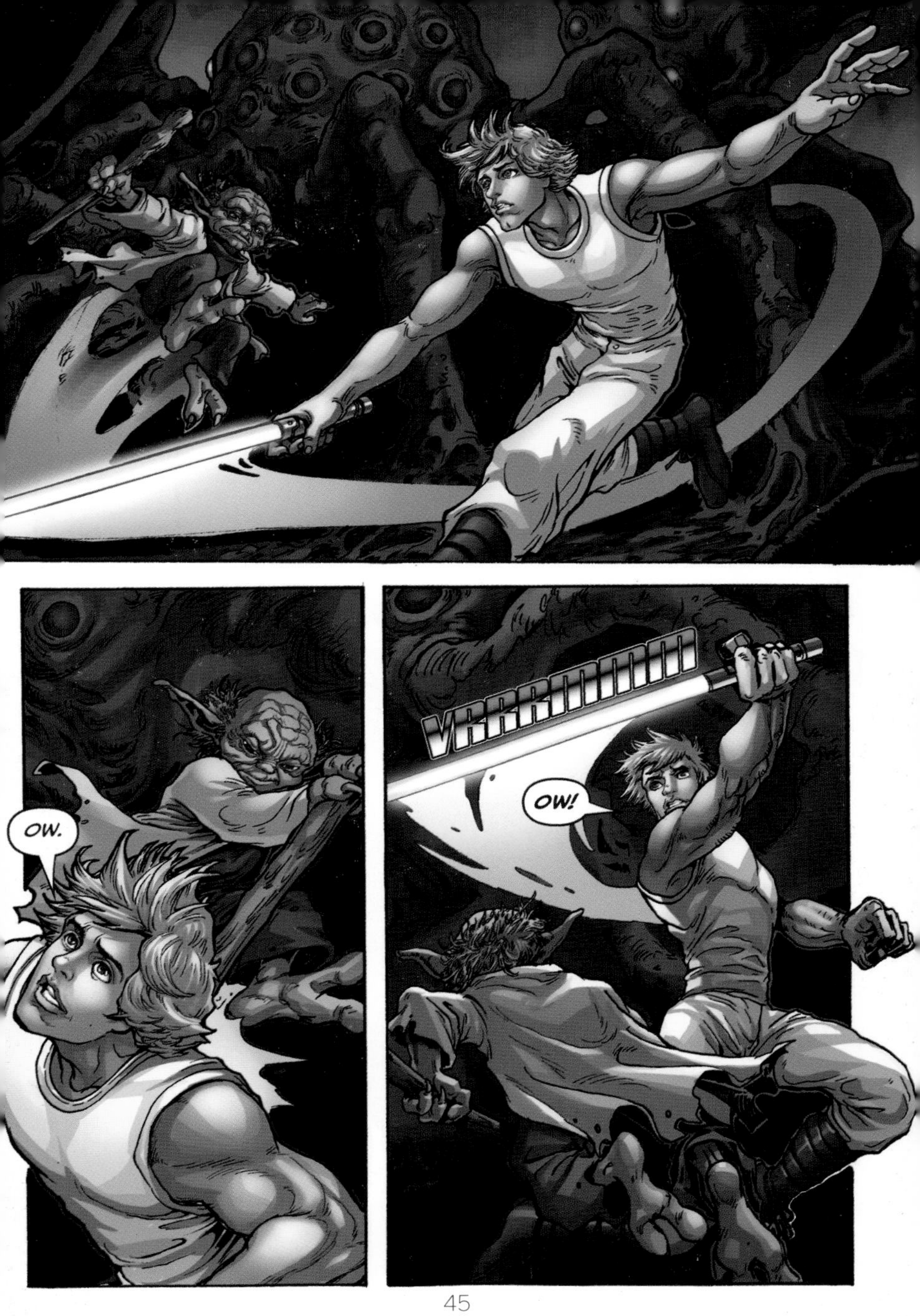
OW.
VRRRMMM
OW!

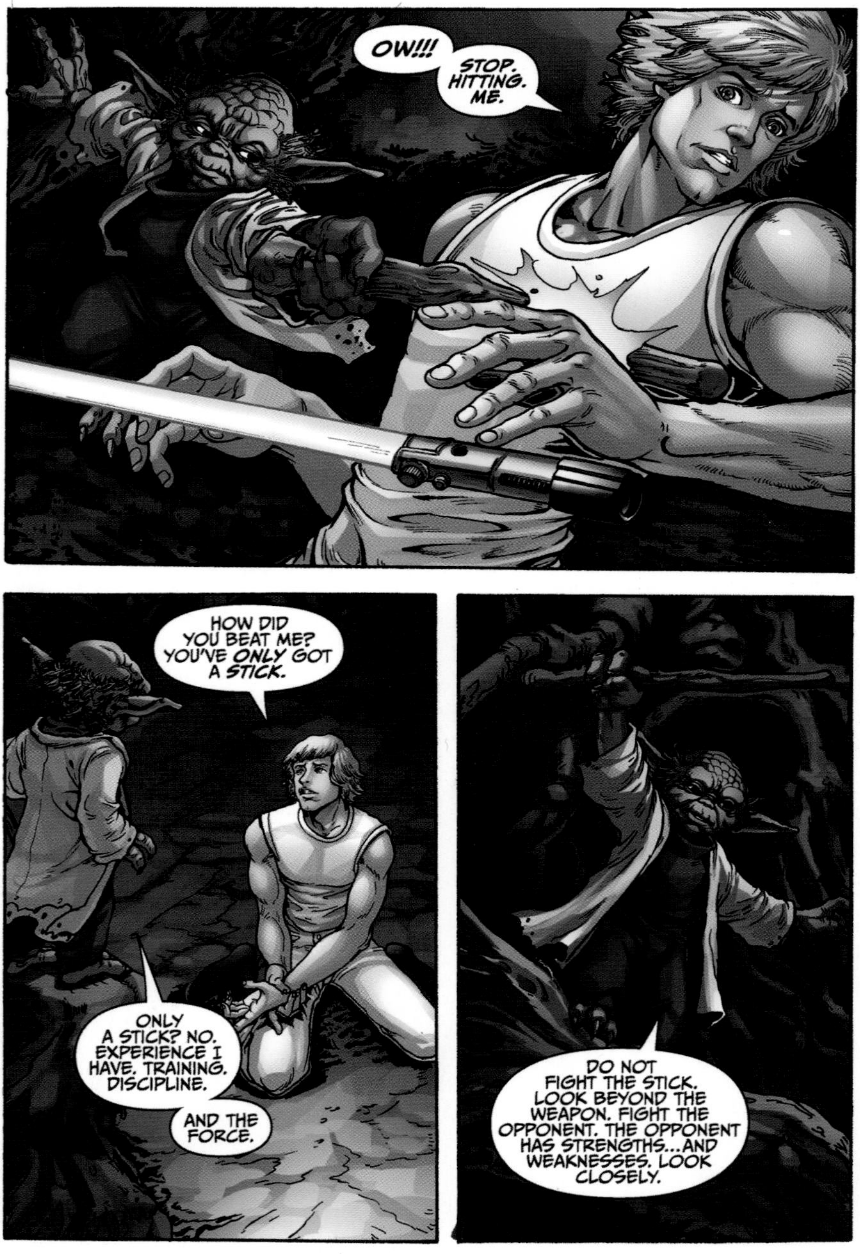
OW!!!
STOP. HITTING. ME.
HOW DID YOU BEAT ME? YOU'VE *ONLY* GOT A *STICK.*
ONLY A STICK? NO. EXPERIENCE I HAVE. TRAINING. DISCIPLINE.
AND THE FORCE.
DO NOT FIGHT THE STICK. LOOK BEYOND THE WEAPON. FIGHT THE OPPONENT. THE OPPONENT HAS STRENGTHS...AND WEAKNESSES. LOOK CLOSELY.

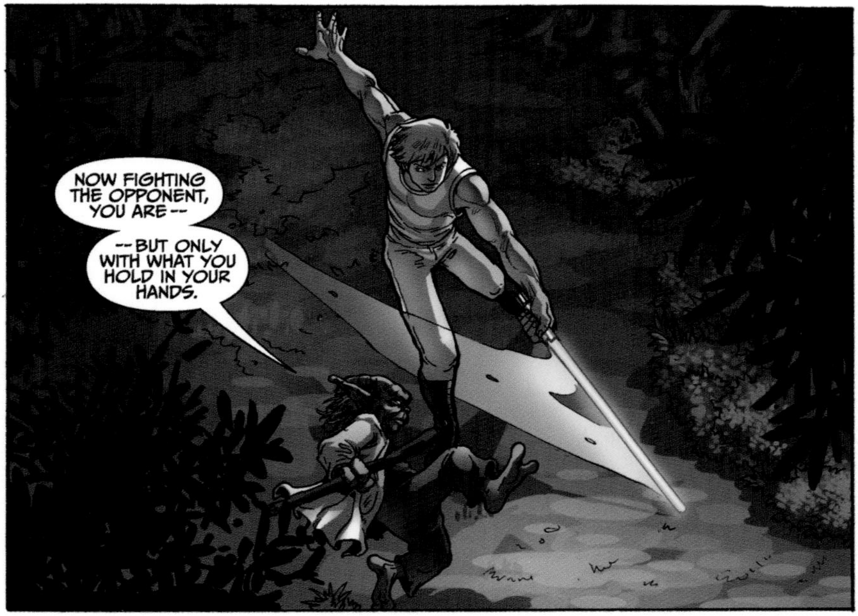
NOW FIGHTING THE OPPONENT, YOU ARE --
-- BUT ONLY WITH WHAT YOU HOLD IN YOUR HANDS.

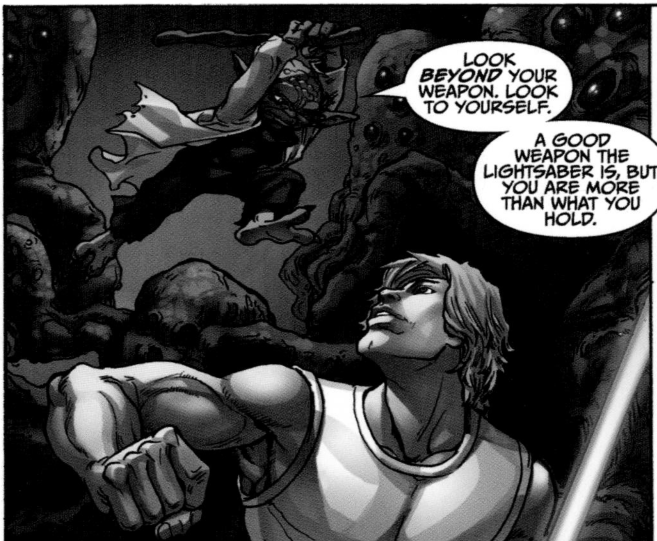
LOOK BEYOND YOUR WEAPON. LOOK TO YOURSELF.
A GOOD WEAPON THE LIGHTSABER IS, BUT YOU ARE MORE THAN WHAT YOU HOLD.

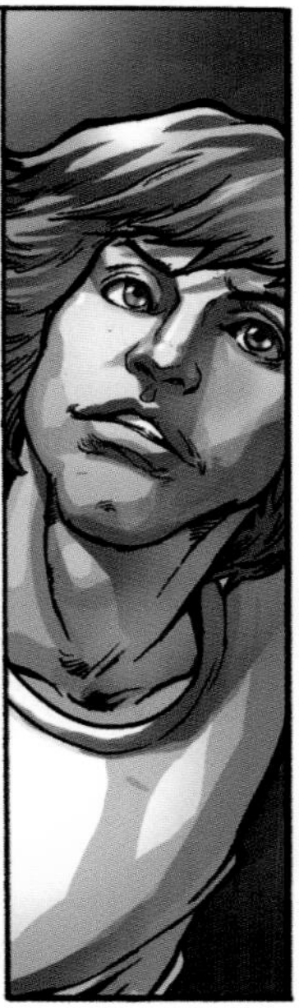

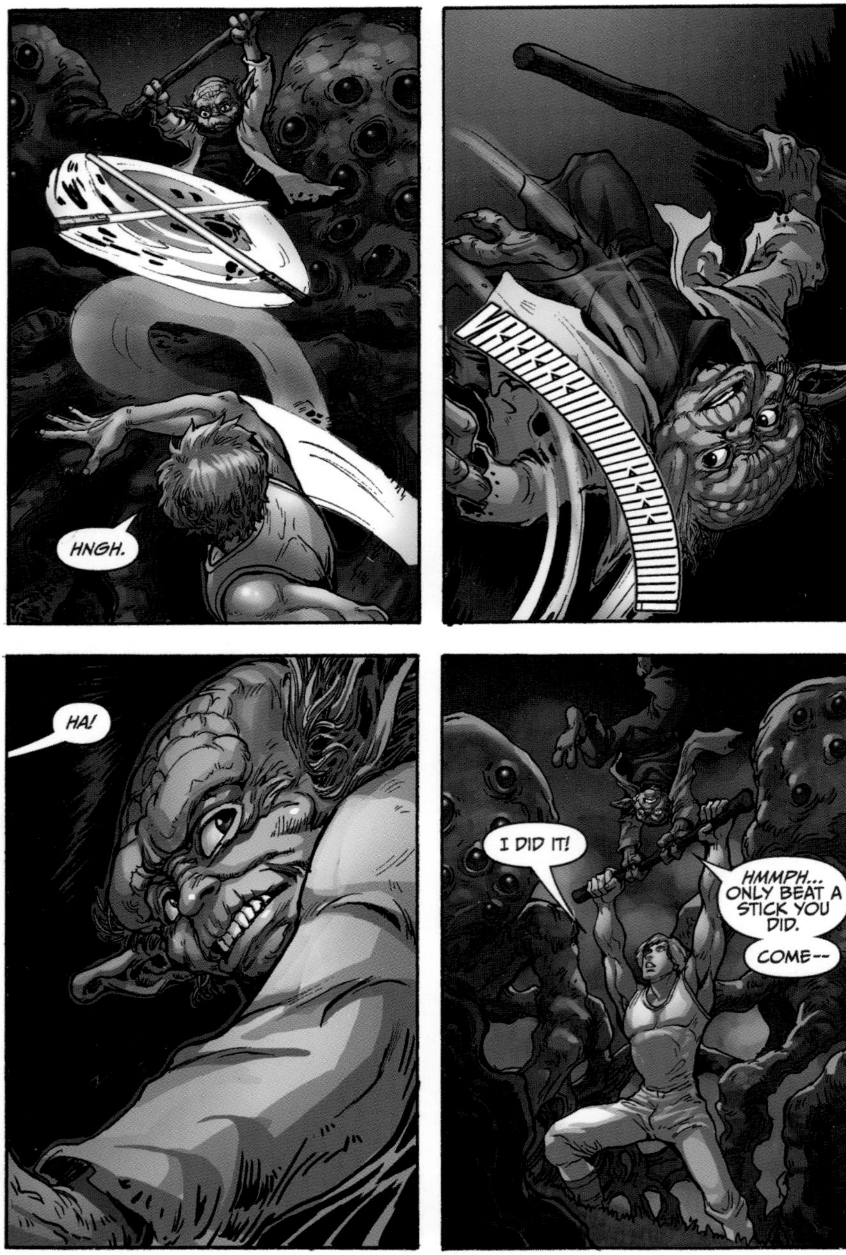
HNGH.
HA!
I DID IT!
HMMPH... ONLY BEAT A STICK YOU DID.
COME--

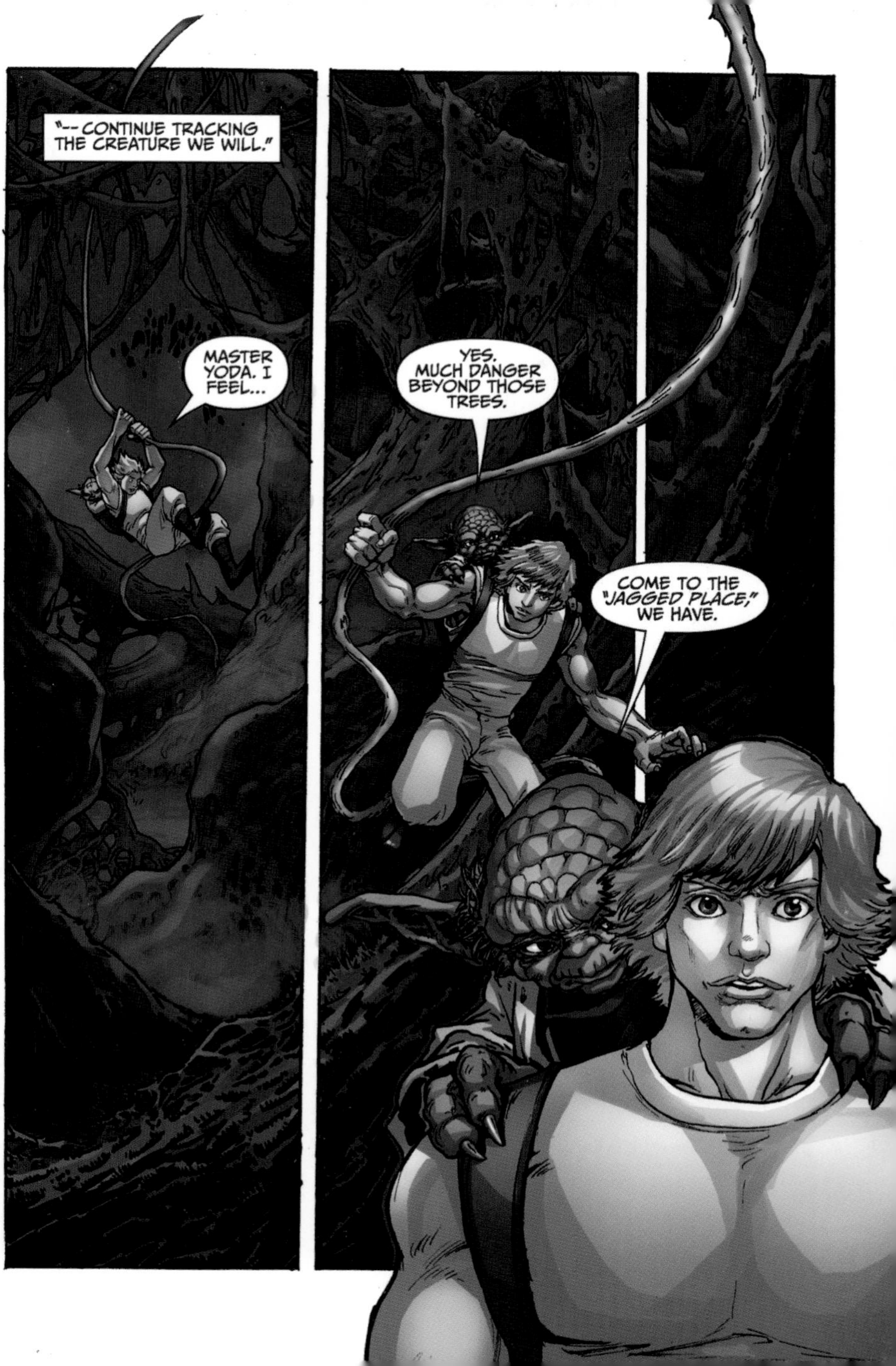
"-- CONTINUE TRACKING THE CREATURE WE WILL."
MASTER YODA. I FEEL...
YES. MUCH DANGER BEYOND THOSE TREES.
COME TO THE "JAGGED PLACE," WE HAVE.

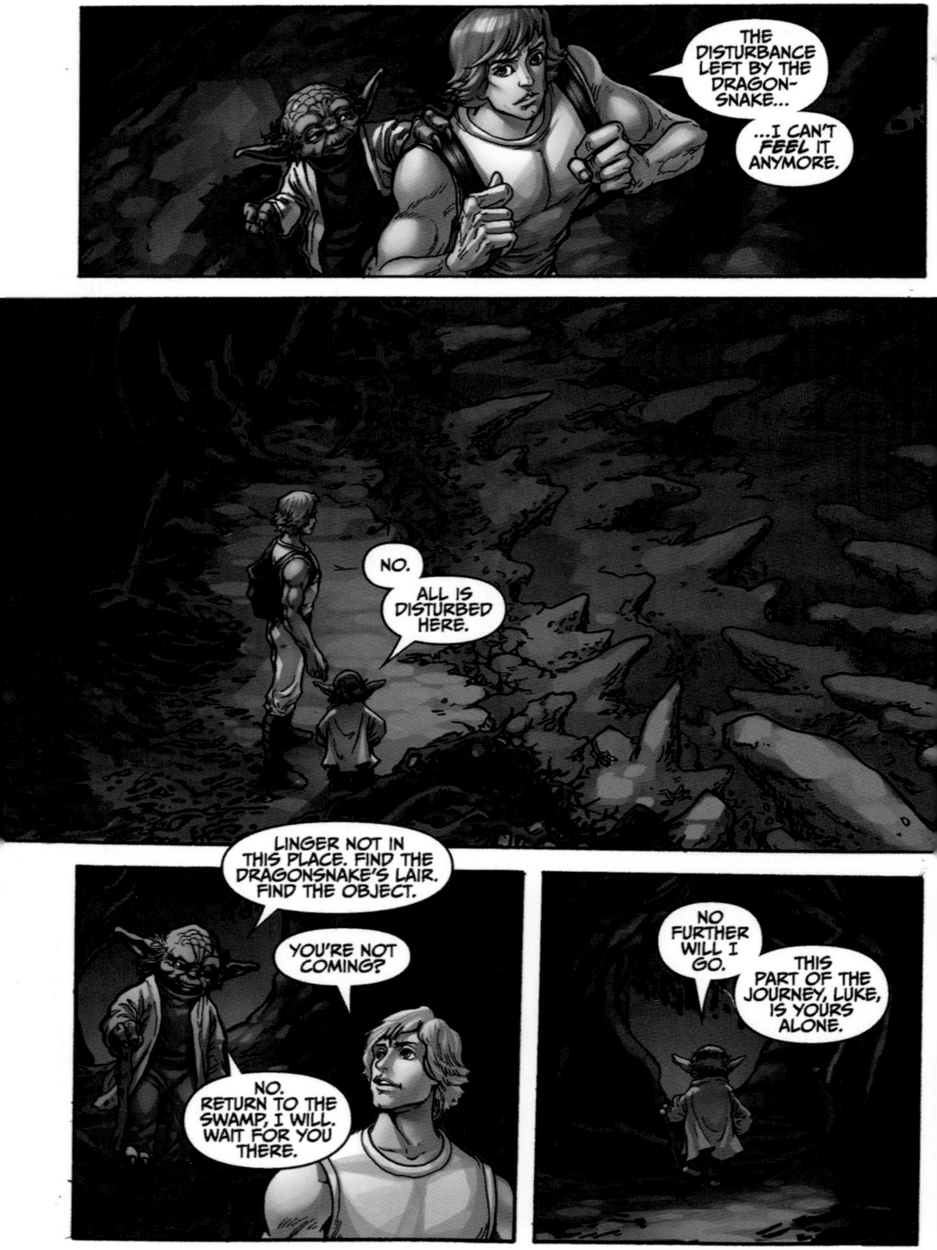
THE DISTURBANCE LEFT BY THE DRAGON-SNAKE...
...I CAN'T *FEEL* IT ANYMORE.
NO.
ALL IS DISTURBED HERE.
LINGER NOT IN THIS PLACE. FIND THE DRAGONSNAKE'S LAIR. FIND THE OBJECT.
YOU'RE NOT COMING?
NO. RETURN TO THE SWAMP, I WILL. WAIT FOR YOU THERE.
NO FURTHER WILL I GO.
THIS PART OF THE JOURNEY, LUKE, IS YOURS ALONE.

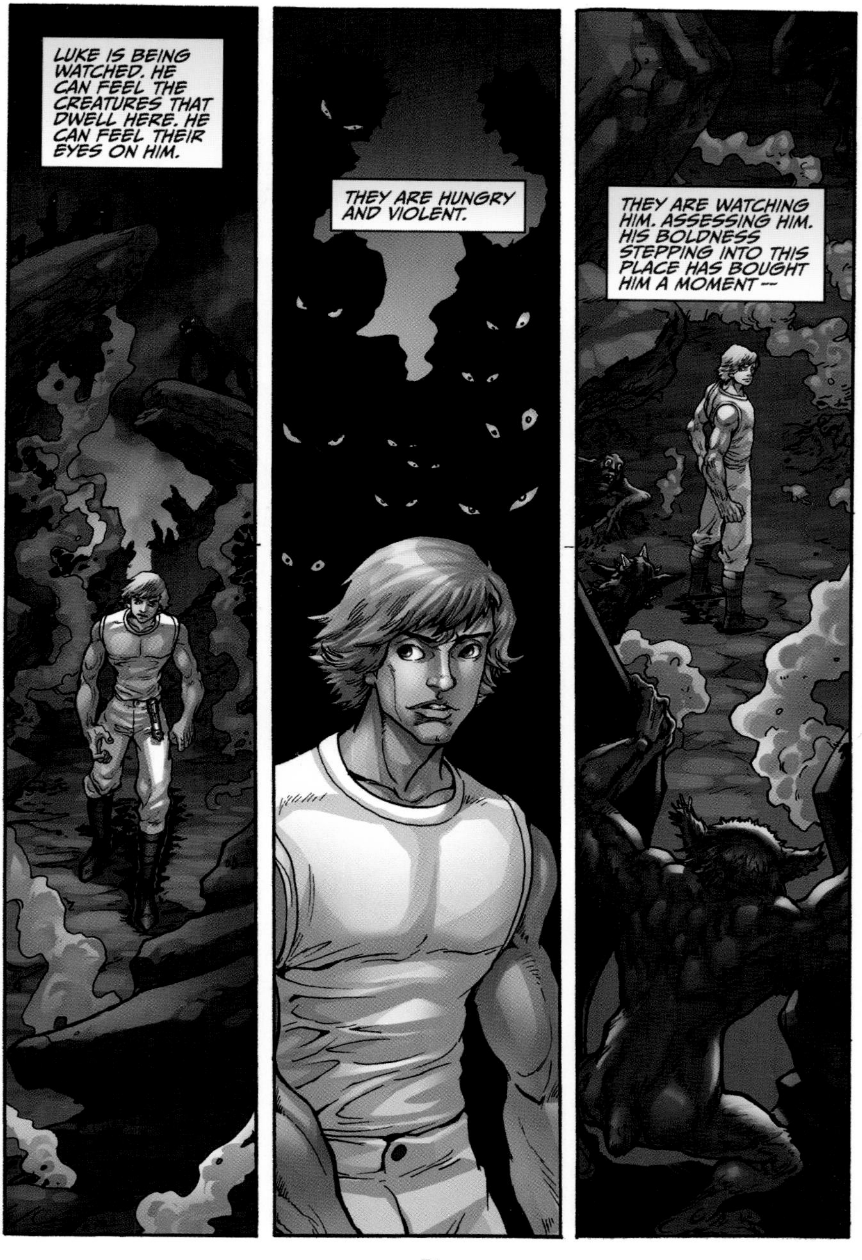
LUKE IS BEING WATCHED. HE CAN FEEL THE CREATURES THAT DWELL HERE. HE CAN FEEL THEIR EYES ON HIM.
THEY ARE HUNGRY AND VIOLENT.
THEY ARE WATCHING HIM. ASSESSING HIM. HIS BOLDNESS STEPPING INTO THIS PLACE HAS BOUGHT HIM A MOMENT--

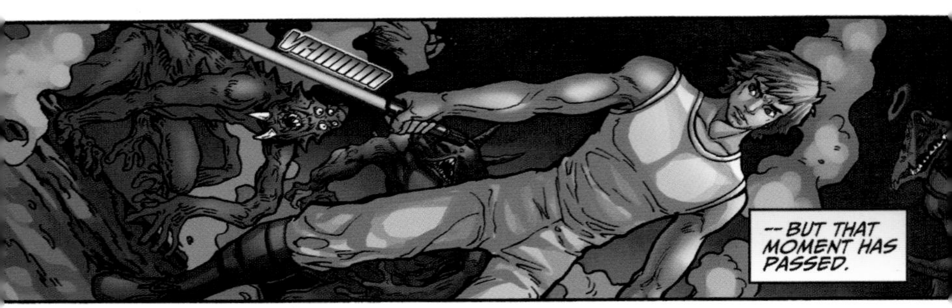
-- BUT THAT MOMENT HAS PASSED.

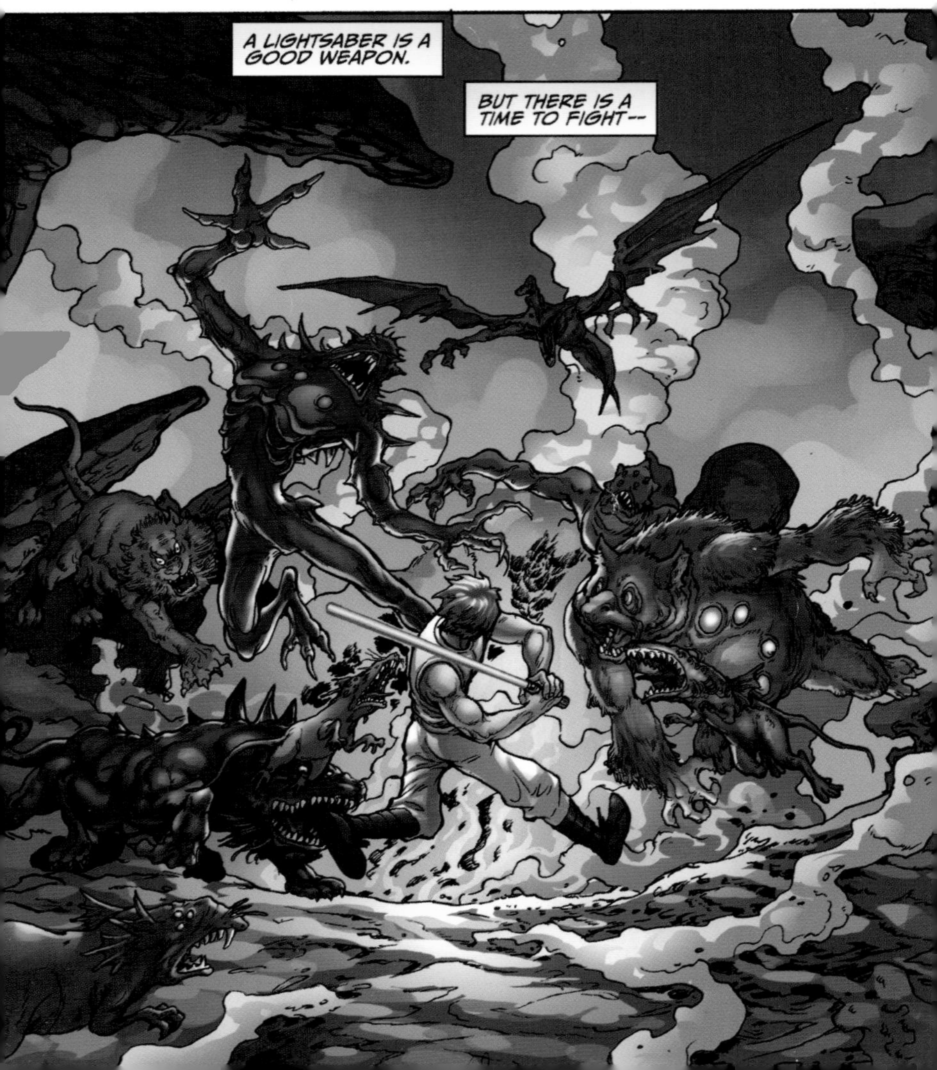
A LIGHTSABER IS A GOOD WEAPON.
BUT THERE IS A TIME TO FIGHT--

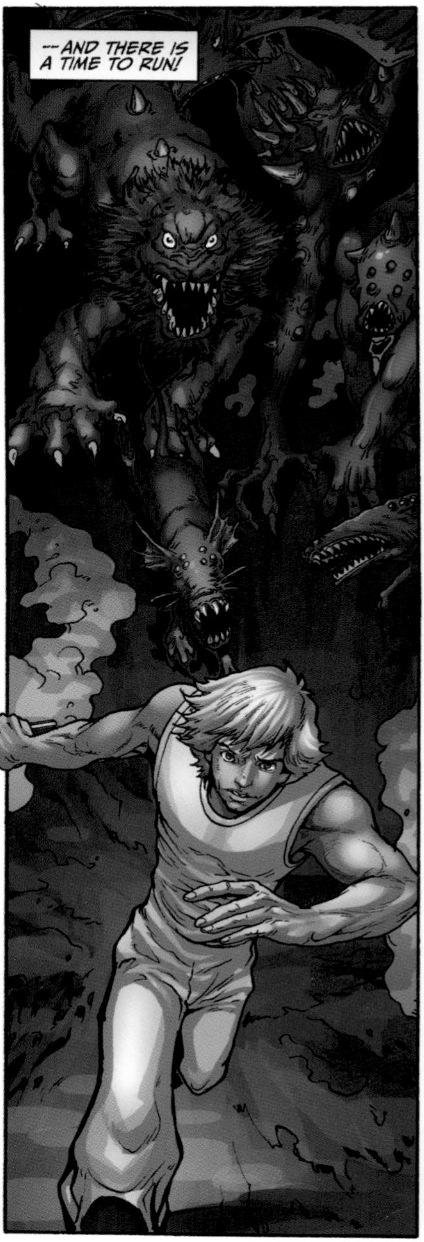
--AND THERE IS A TIME TO RUN!

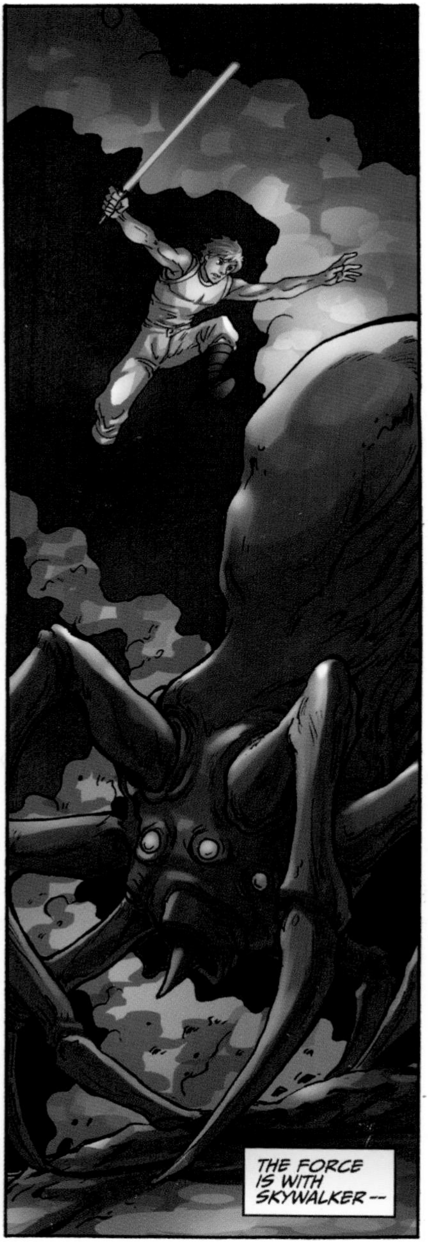
THE FORCE IS WITH SKYWALKER--

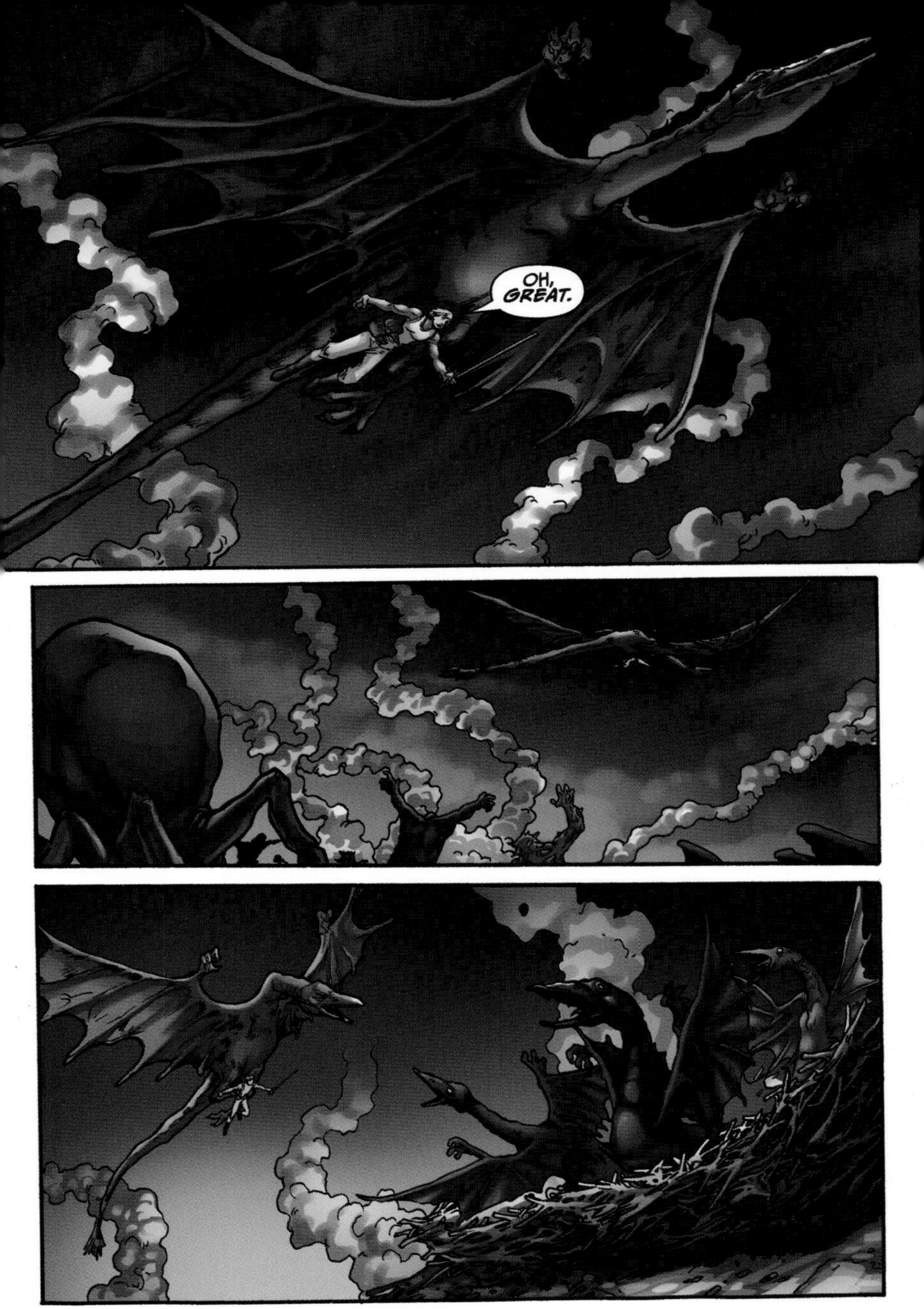
OH, GREAT.

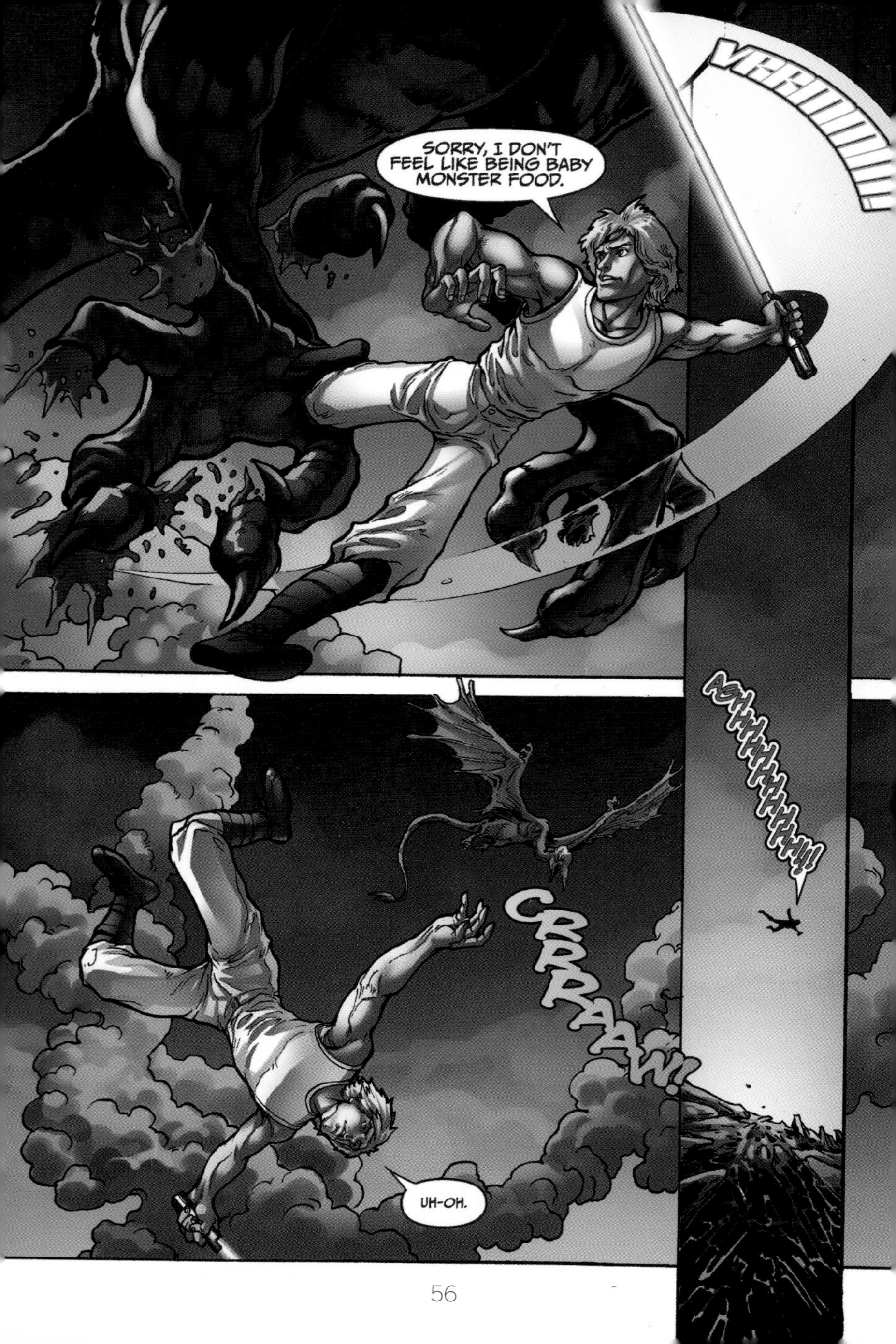
SORRY, I DON'T FEEL LIKE BEING BABY MONSTER FOOD.
AAHHHHHHHHH!!!
CRRAAW!!
UH-OH.

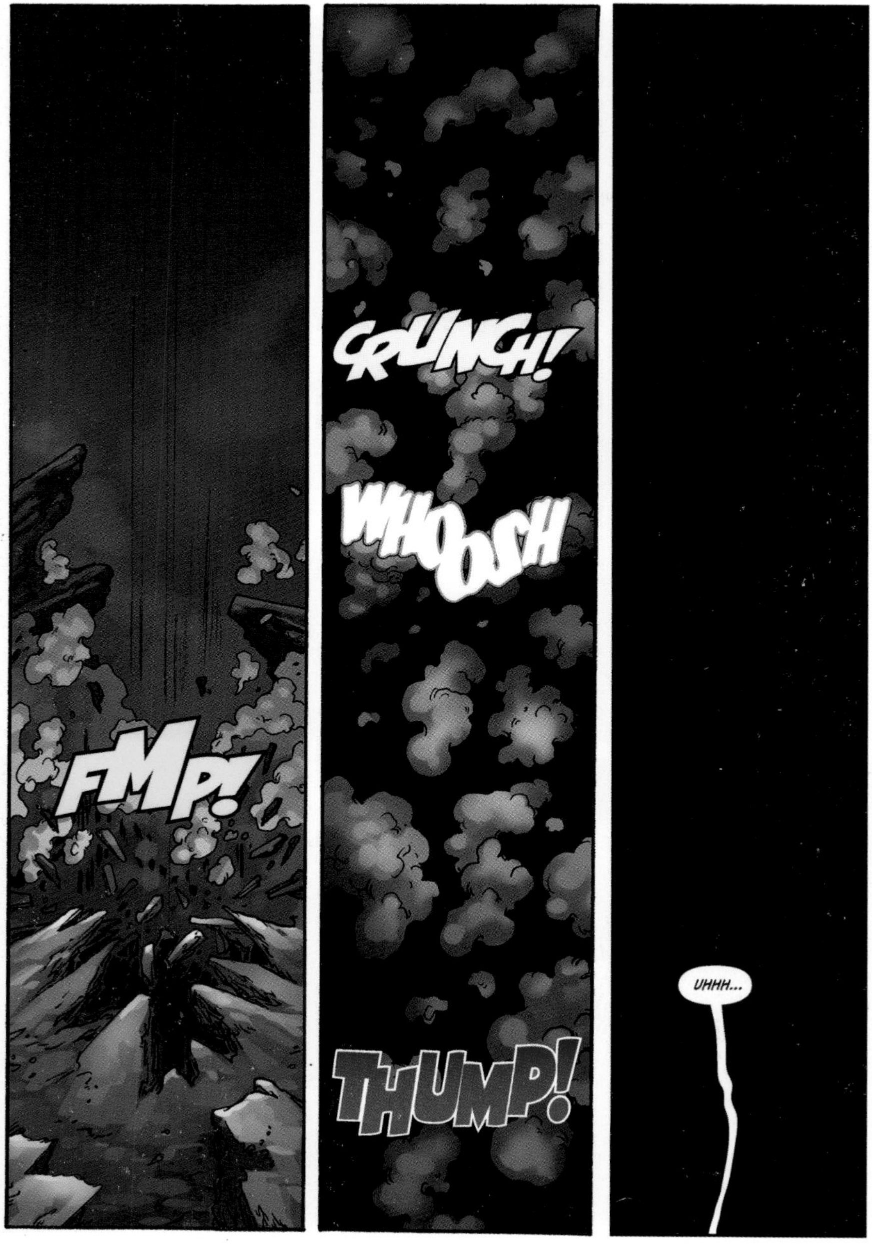
FMP!
CRUNCH!
WHOOOSH
THUMP!
UHHH...

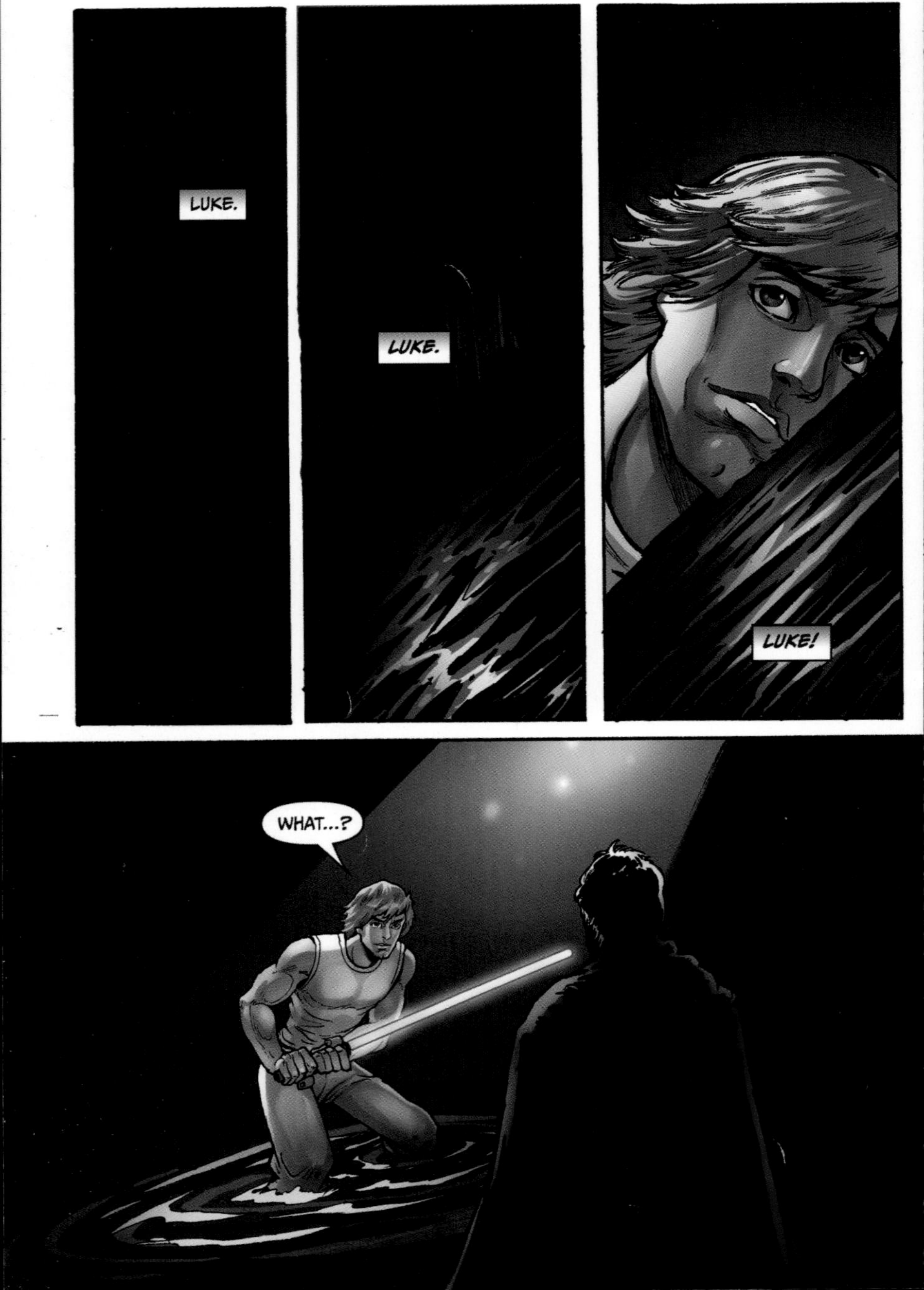
LUKE.
LUKE.
LUKE!
WHAT...?

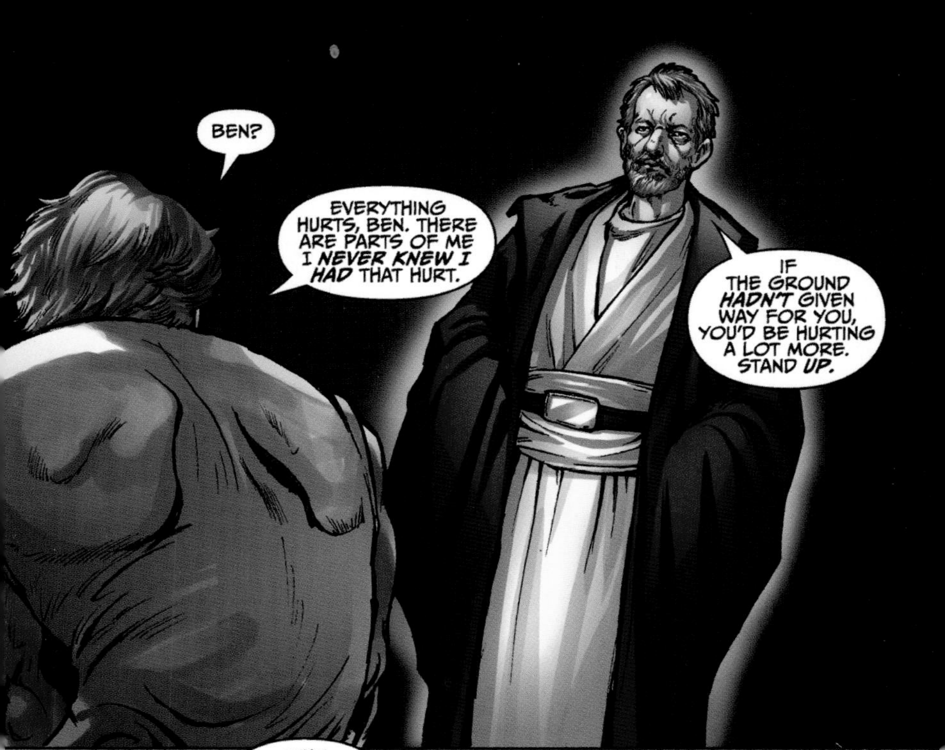
BEN?
EVERYTHING HURTS, BEN. THERE ARE PARTS OF ME I **NEVER KNEW I HAD** THAT HURT.
IF THE GROUND **HADN'T** GIVEN WAY FOR YOU, YOU'D BE HURTING A LOT MORE. STAND **UP.**

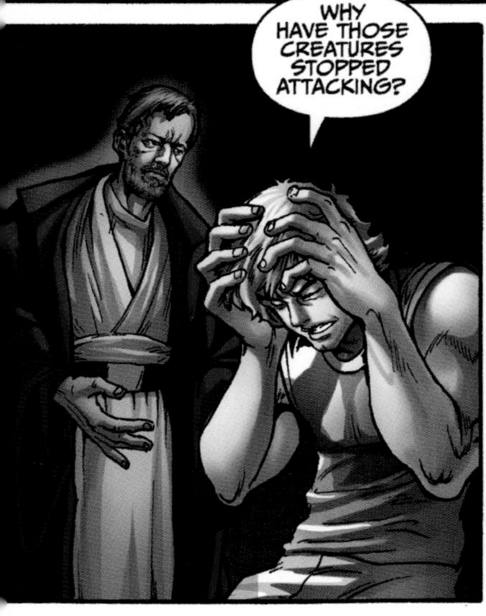
WHY HAVE THOSE CREATURES STOPPED ATTACKING?

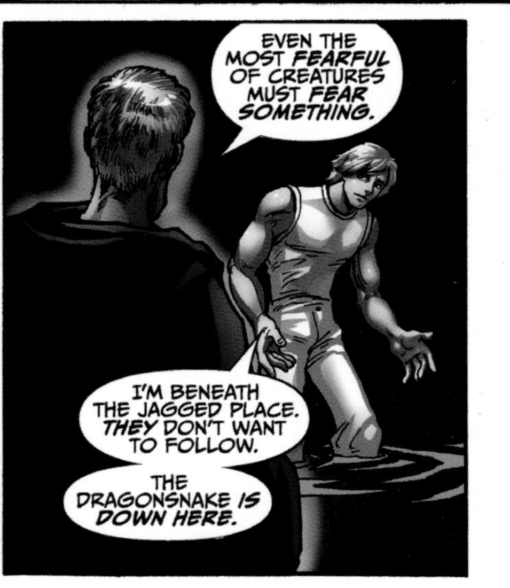
EVEN THE MOST **FEARFUL** OF CREATURES MUST **FEAR SOMETHING.**
I'M BENEATH THE JAGGED PLACE. **THEY** DON'T WANT TO FOLLOW.
THE DRAGONSNAKE **IS DOWN HERE.**

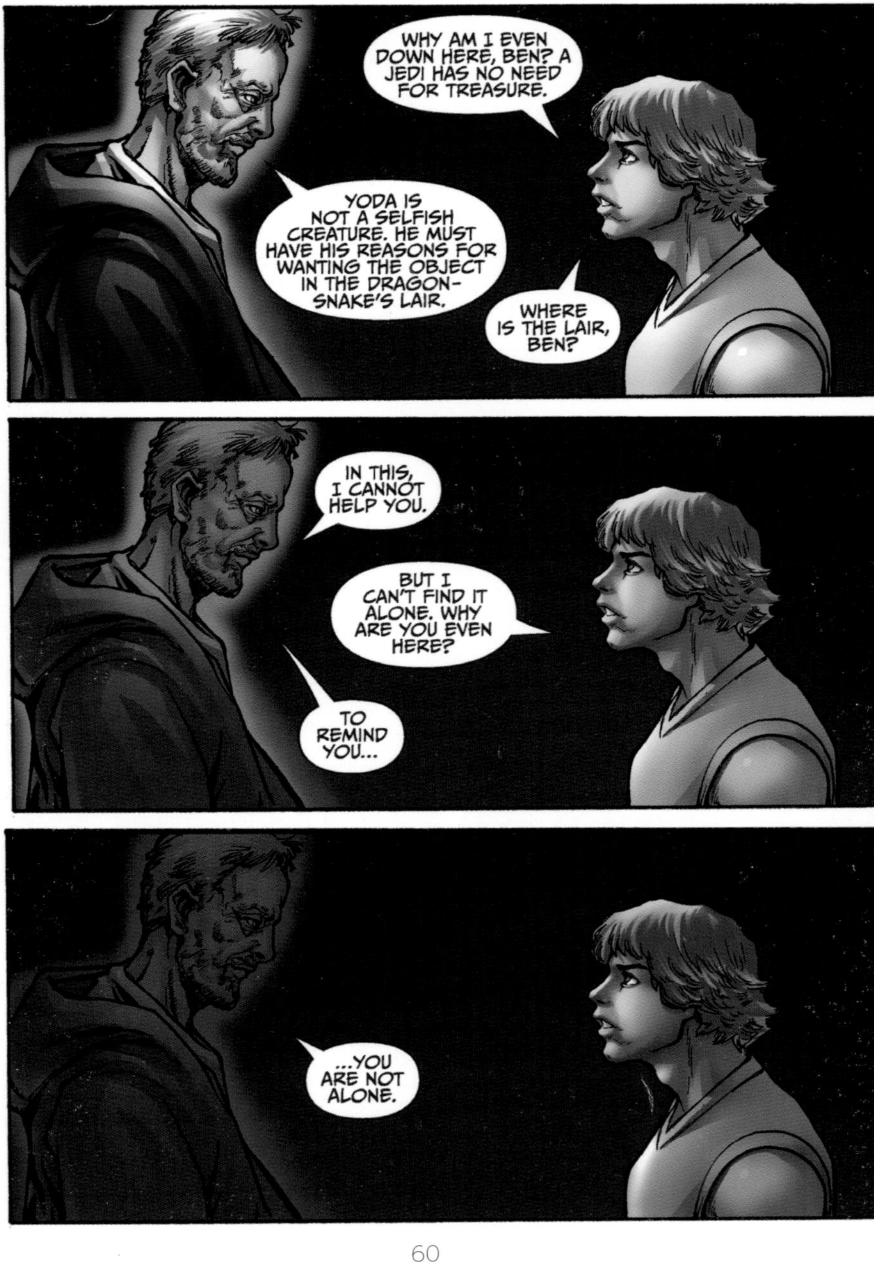
WHY AM I EVEN DOWN HERE, BEN? A JEDI HAS NO NEED FOR TREASURE.
YODA IS NOT A SELFISH CREATURE. HE MUST HAVE HIS REASONS FOR WANTING THE OBJECT IN THE DRAGON-SNAKE'S LAIR.
WHERE IS THE LAIR, BEN?
IN THIS, I CANNOT HELP YOU.
BUT I CAN'T FIND IT ALONE. WHY ARE YOU EVEN HERE?
TO REMIND YOU...
...YOU ARE NOT ALONE.

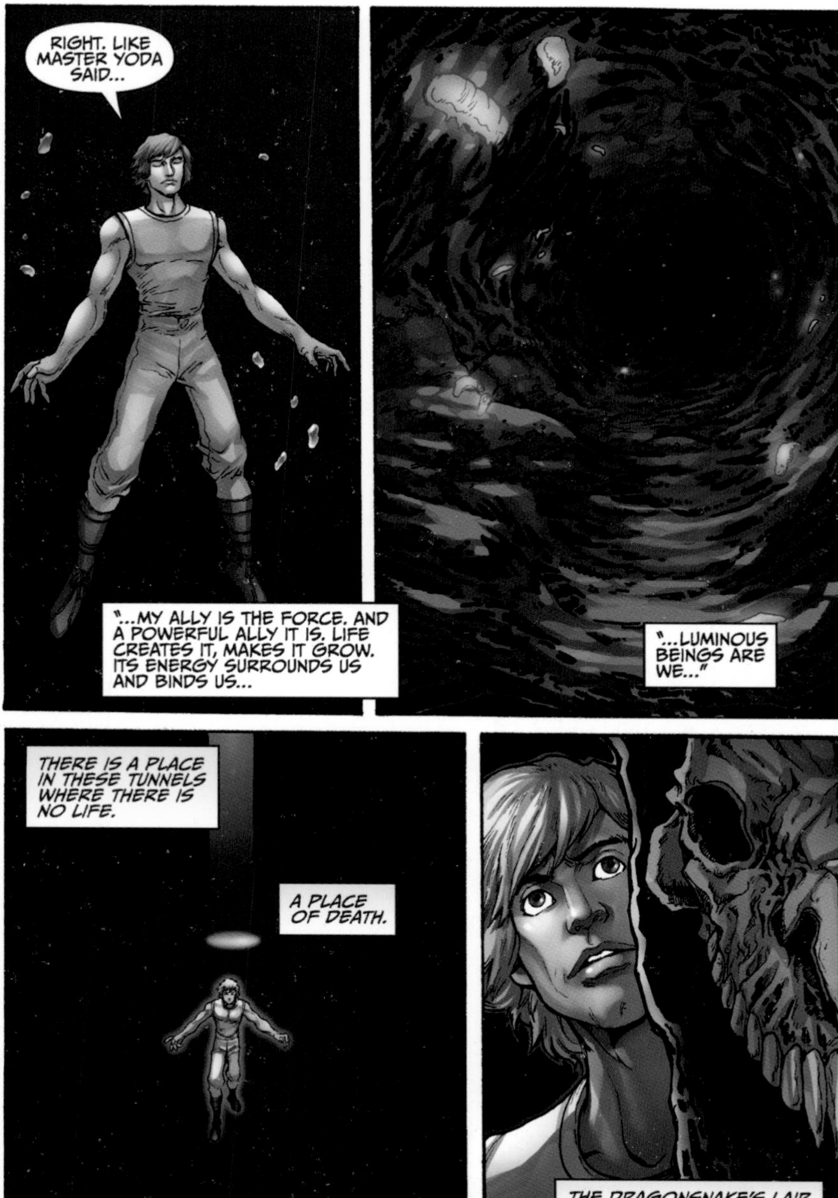
RIGHT. LIKE MASTER YODA SAID...
"...MY ALLY IS THE FORCE. AND A POWERFUL ALLY IT IS. LIFE CREATES IT, MAKES IT GROW. ITS ENERGY SURROUNDS US AND BINDS US...
"...LUMINOUS BEINGS ARE WE..."
THERE IS A PLACE IN THESE TUNNELS WHERE THERE IS NO LIFE.
A PLACE OF DEATH.
THE DRAGONSNAKE'S LAIR.

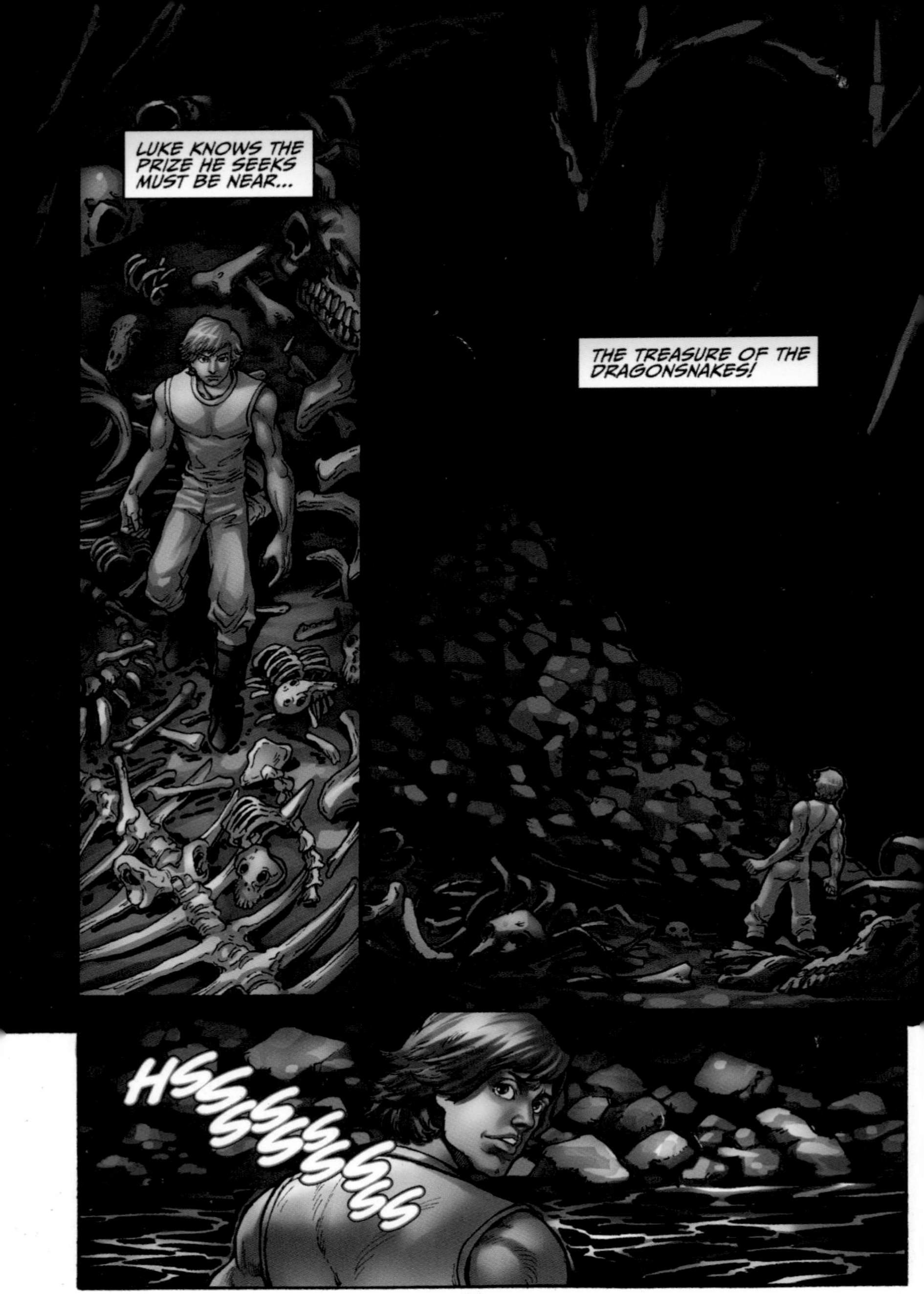
LUKE KNOWS THE PRIZE HE SEEKS MUST BE NEAR...
THE TREASURE OF THE DRAGONSNAKES!
HSSSSSSSSSSS

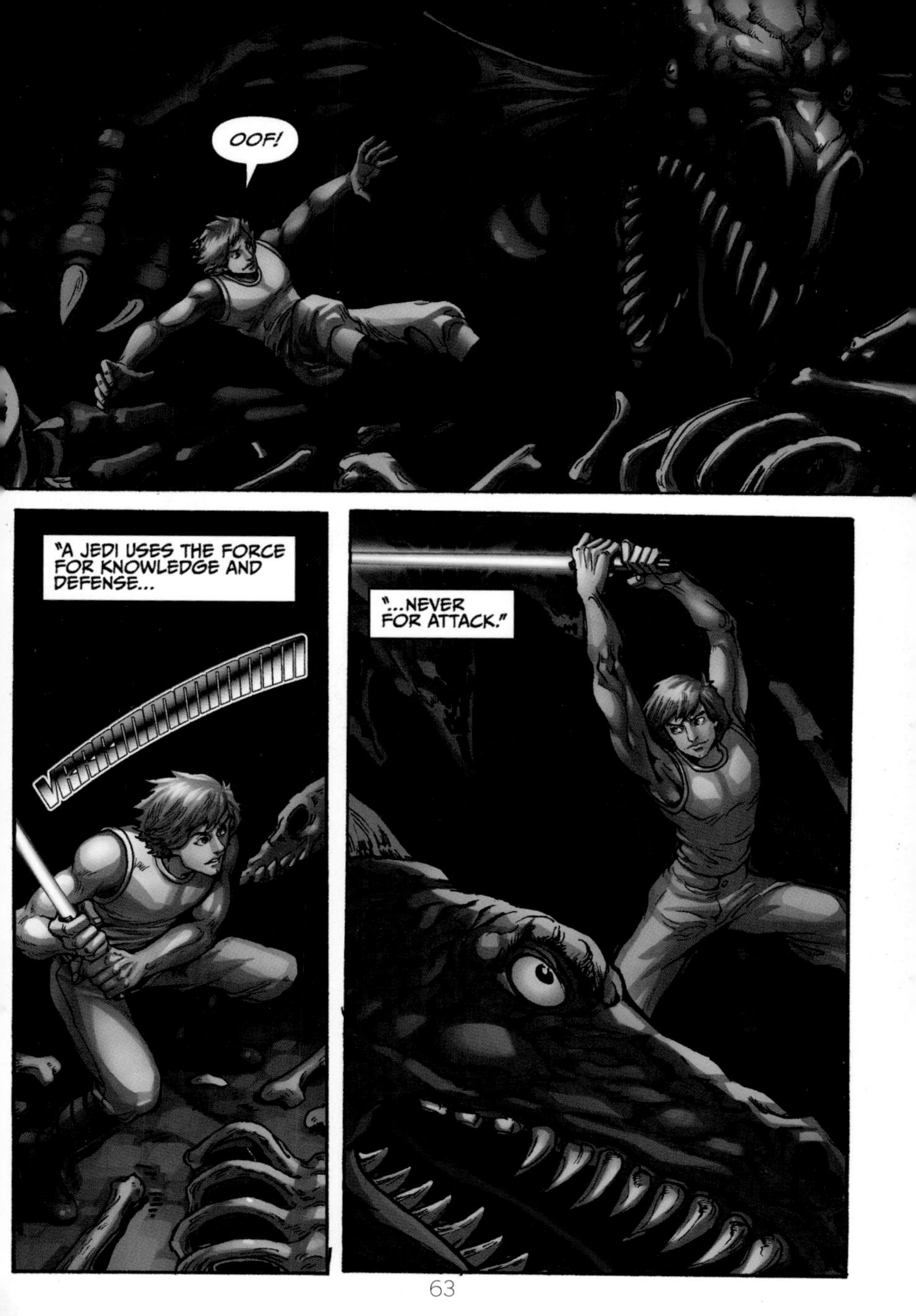
OOF!
"A JEDI USES THE FORCE FOR KNOWLEDGE AND DEFENSE...
"...NEVER FOR ATTACK."

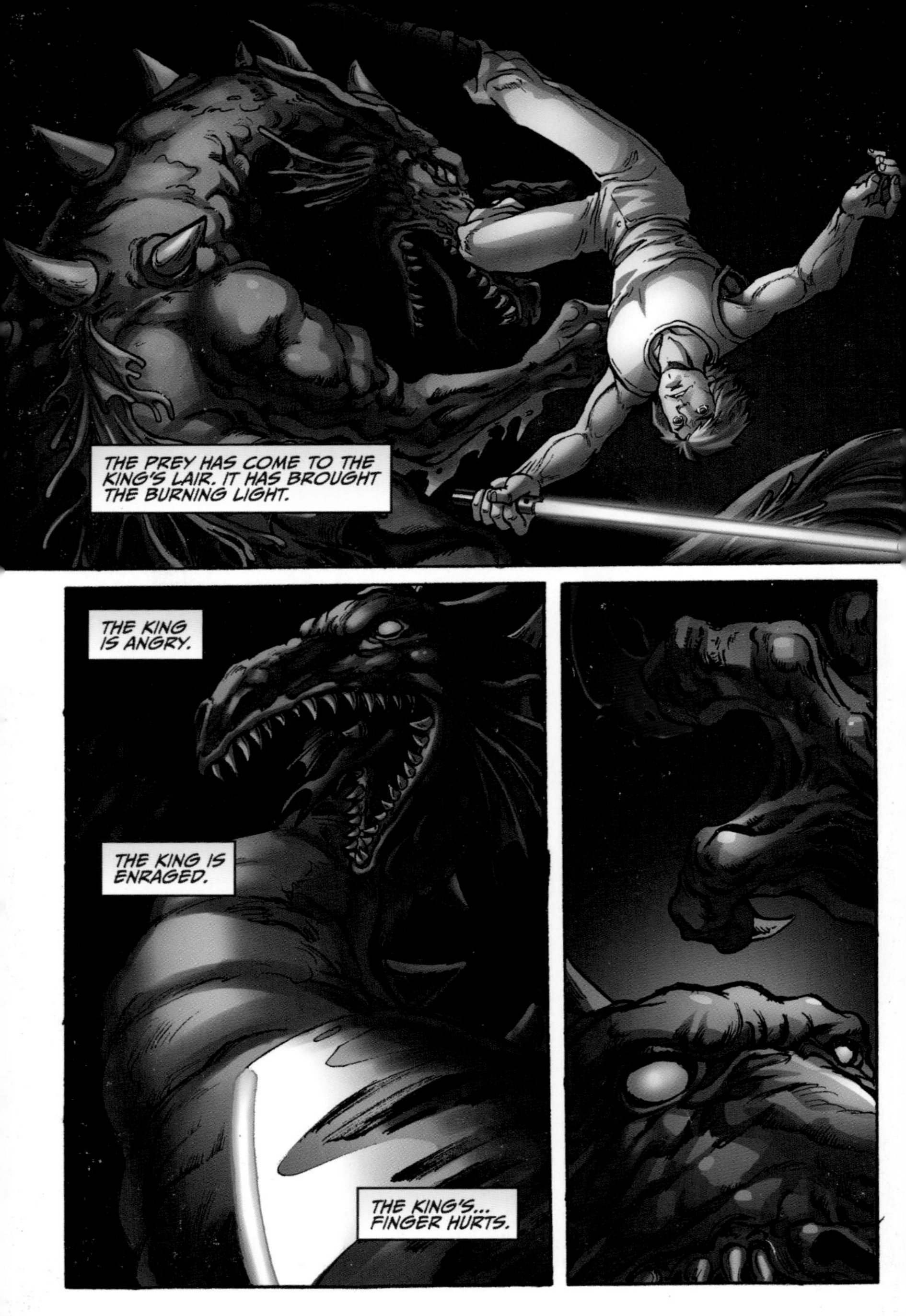
THE PREY HAS COME TO THE KING'S LAIR. IT HAS BROUGHT THE BURNING LIGHT.
THE KING IS ANGRY.
THE KING IS ENRAGED.
THE KING'S... FINGER HURTS.

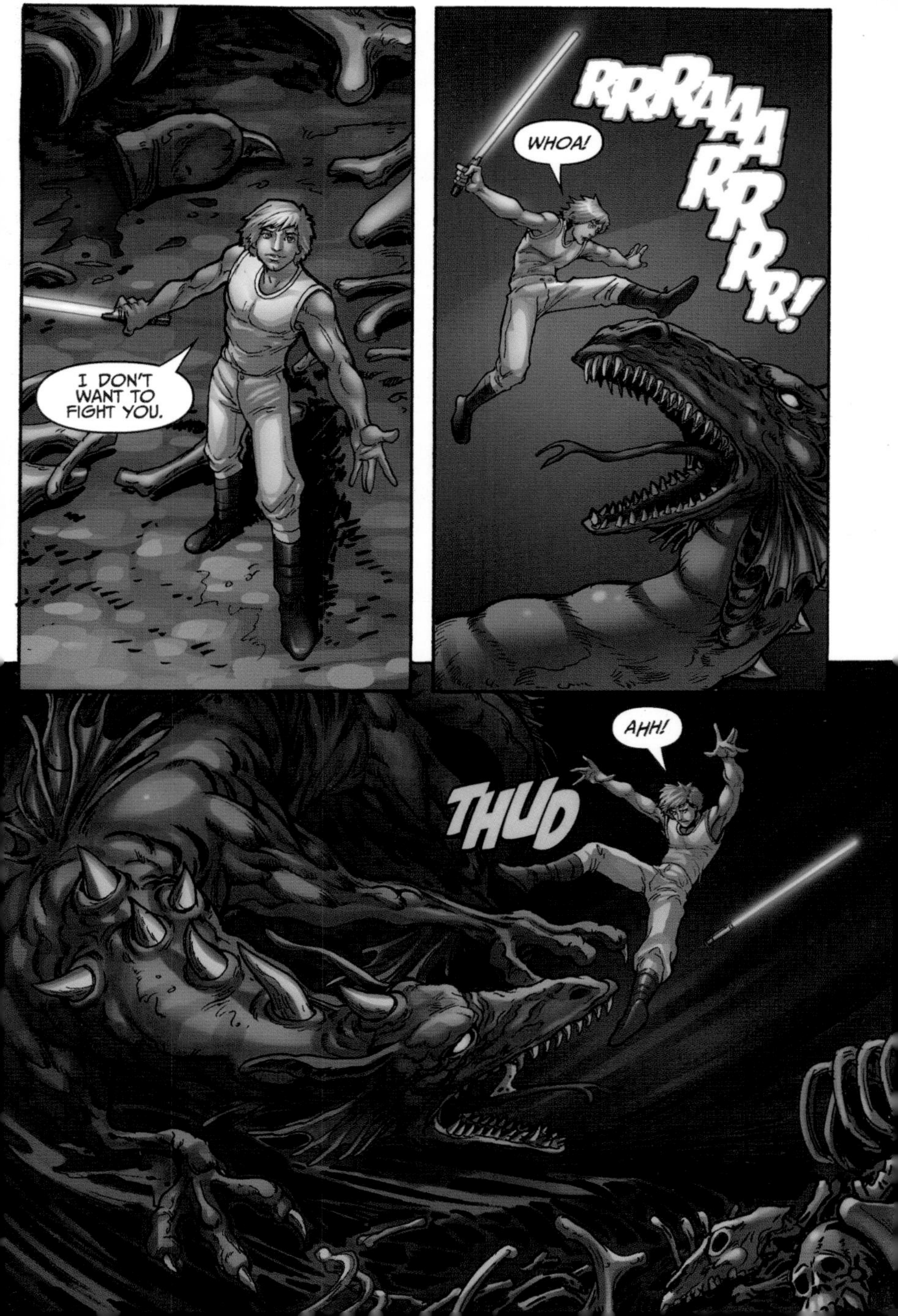
I DON'T WANT TO FIGHT YOU.
WHOA!
RRRRAAAARRRRR!
THUD
AHH!

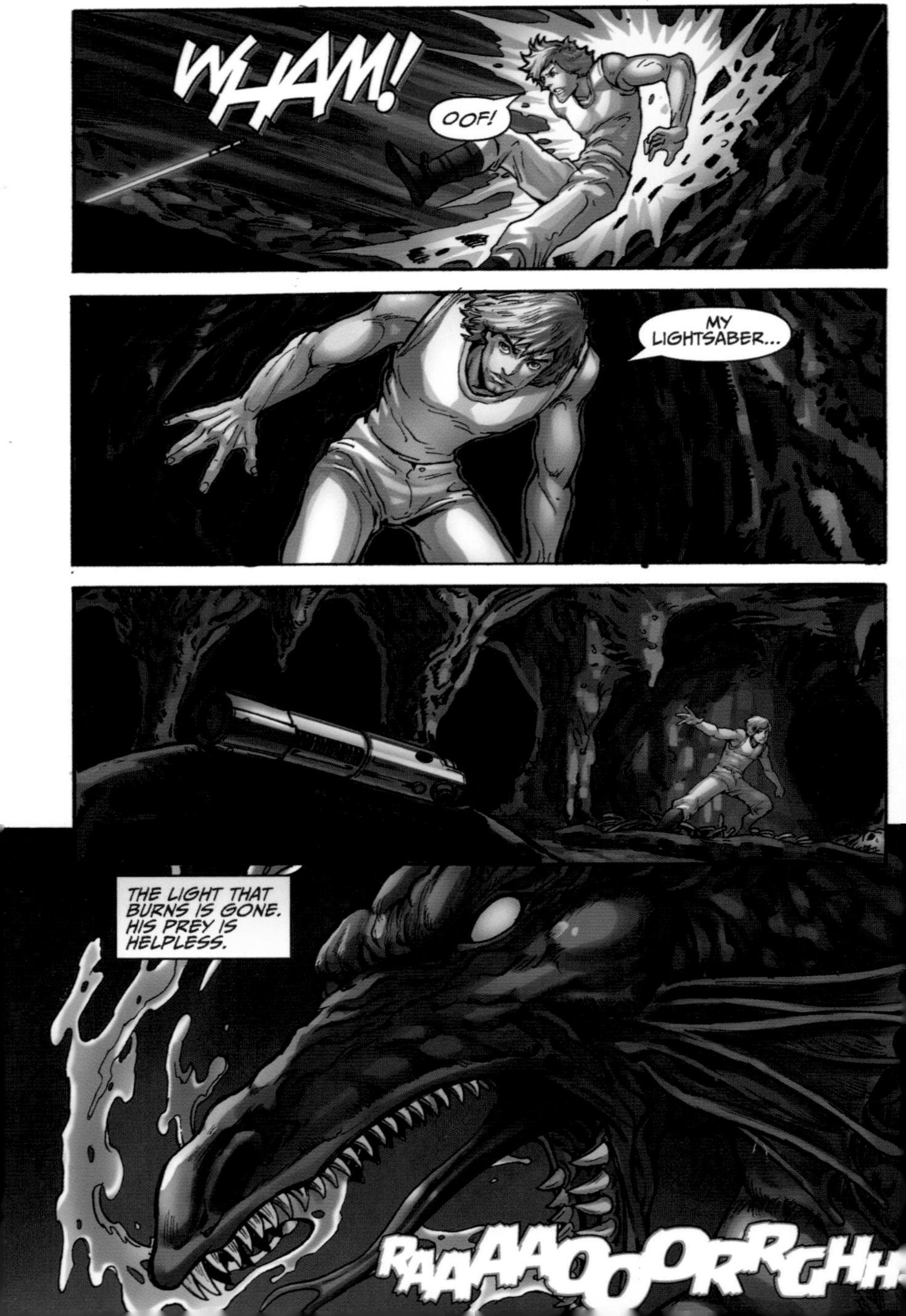
WHAM!
OOF!
MY LIGHTSABER...
THE LIGHT THAT BURNS IS GONE. HIS PREY IS HELPLESS.
RAAAAAOOORRGHH

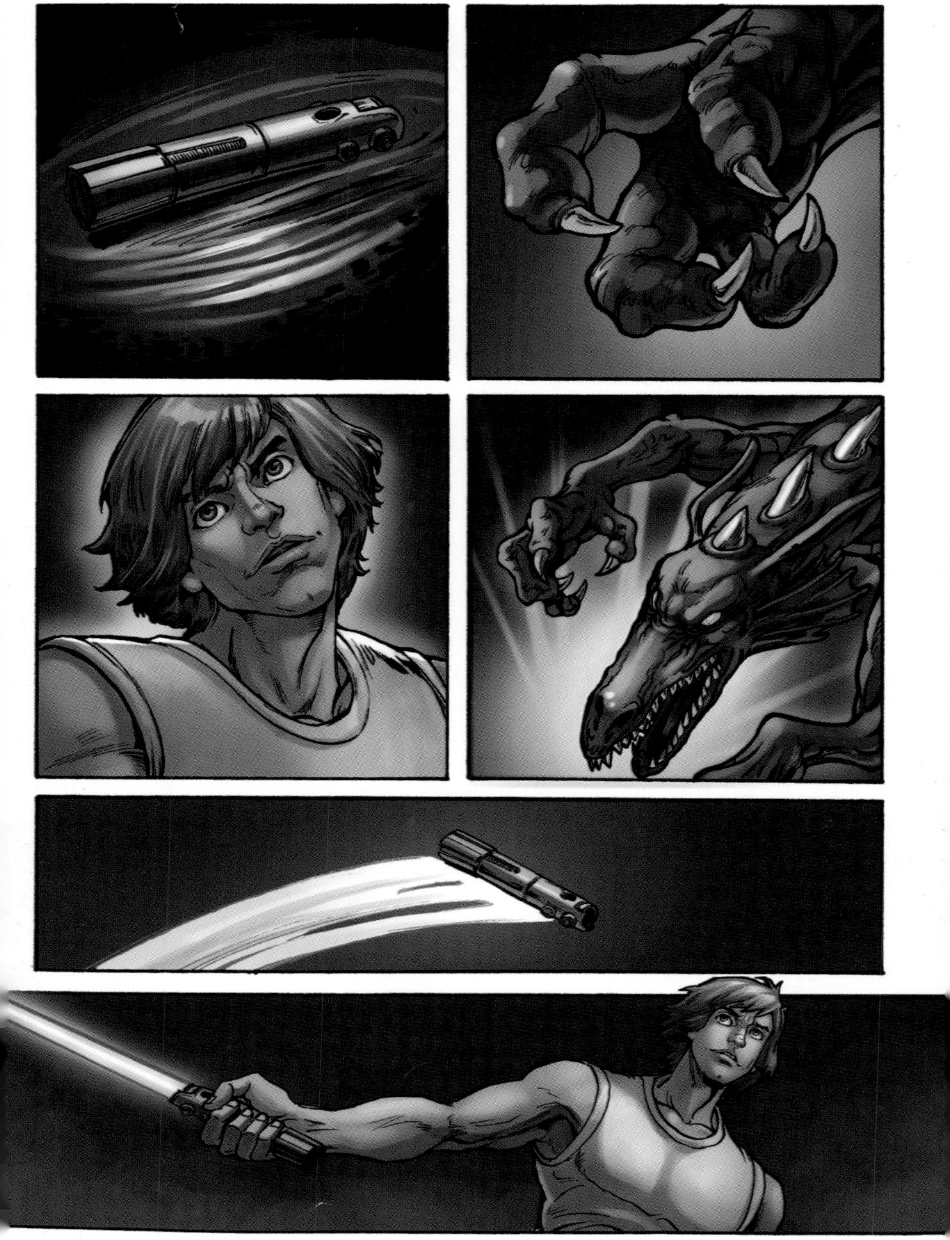

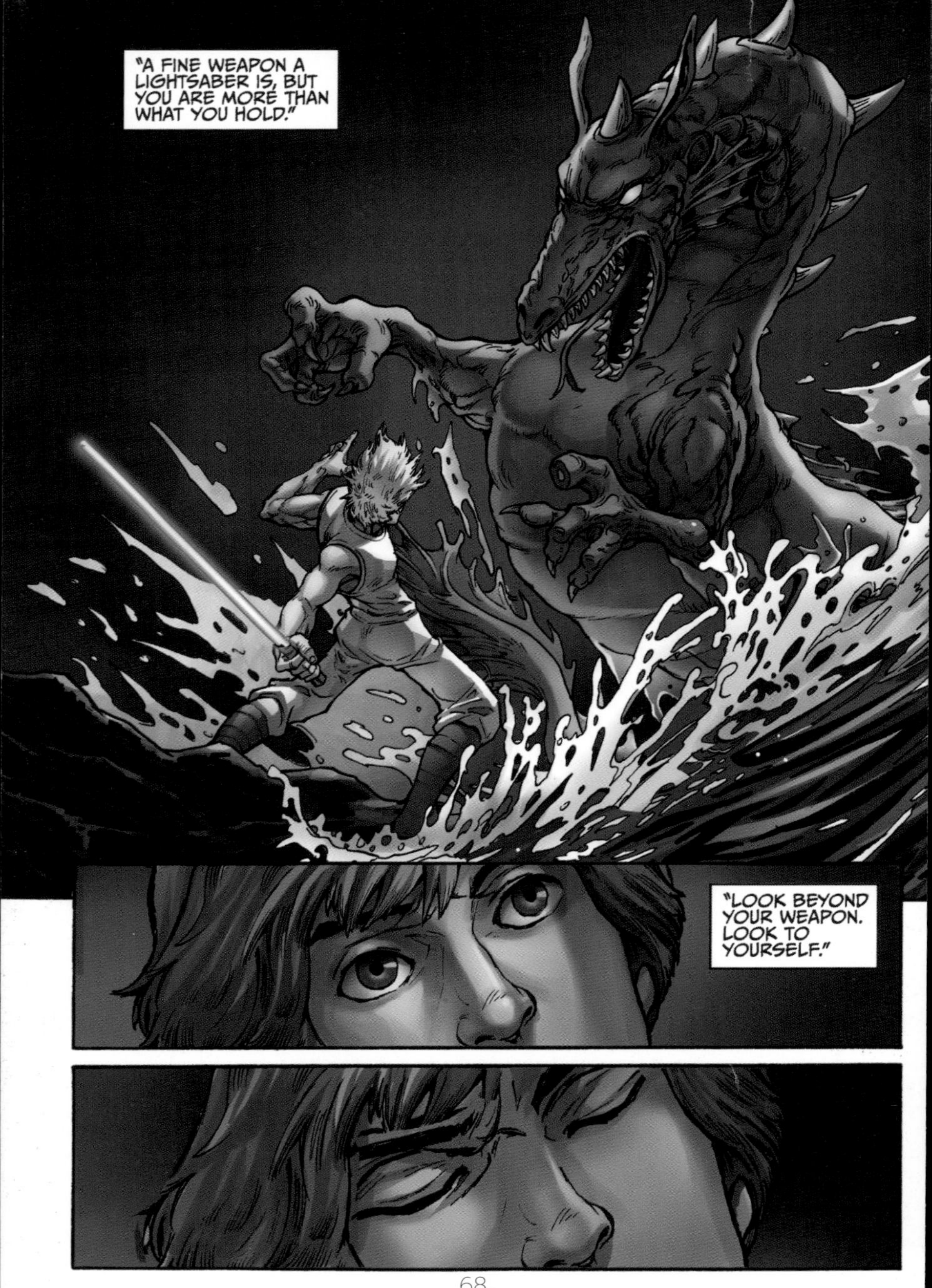
"A FINE WEAPON A LIGHTSABER IS, BUT YOU ARE MORE THAN WHAT YOU HOLD."
"LOOK BEYOND YOUR WEAPON. LOOK TO YOURSELF."

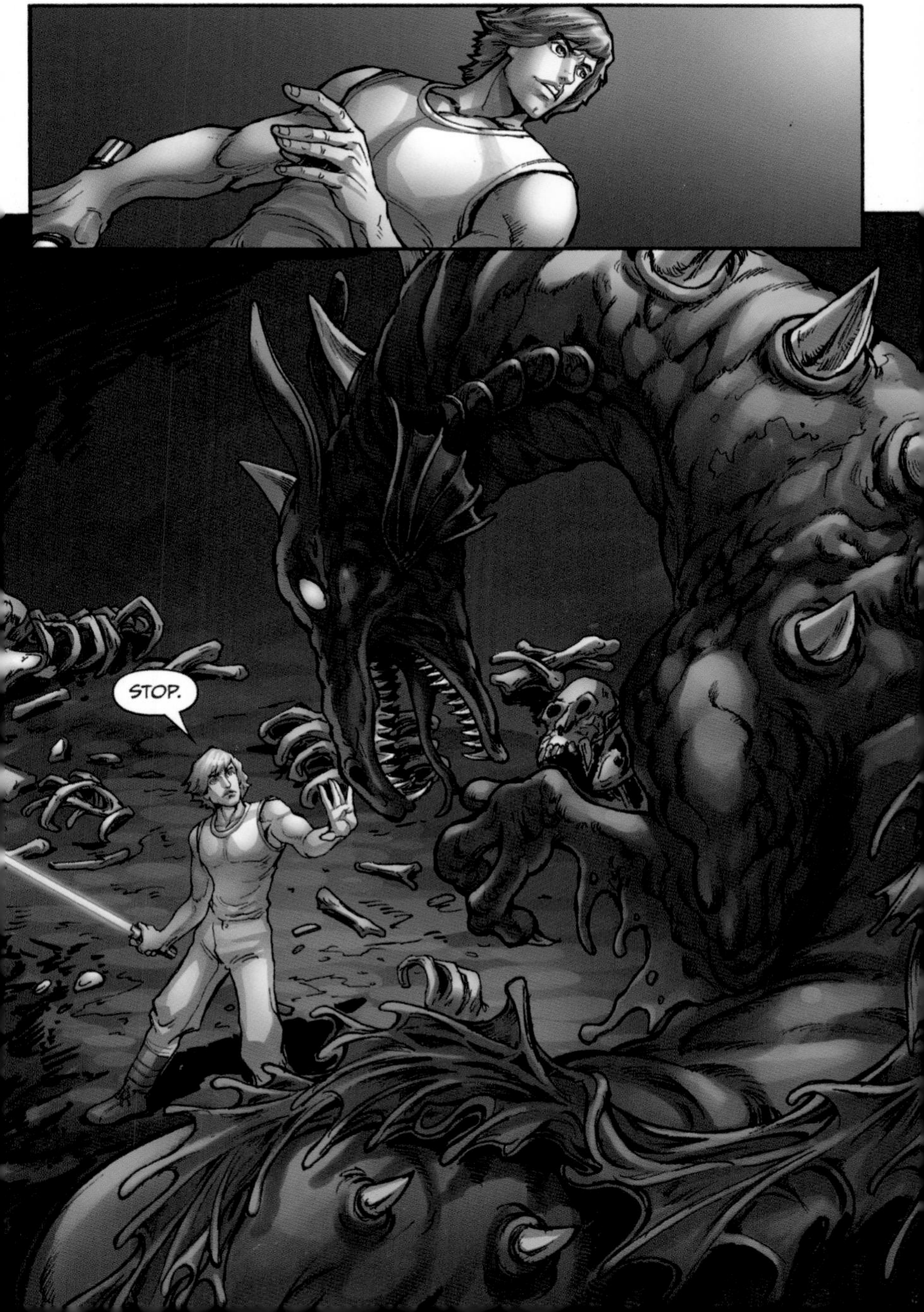
STOP.

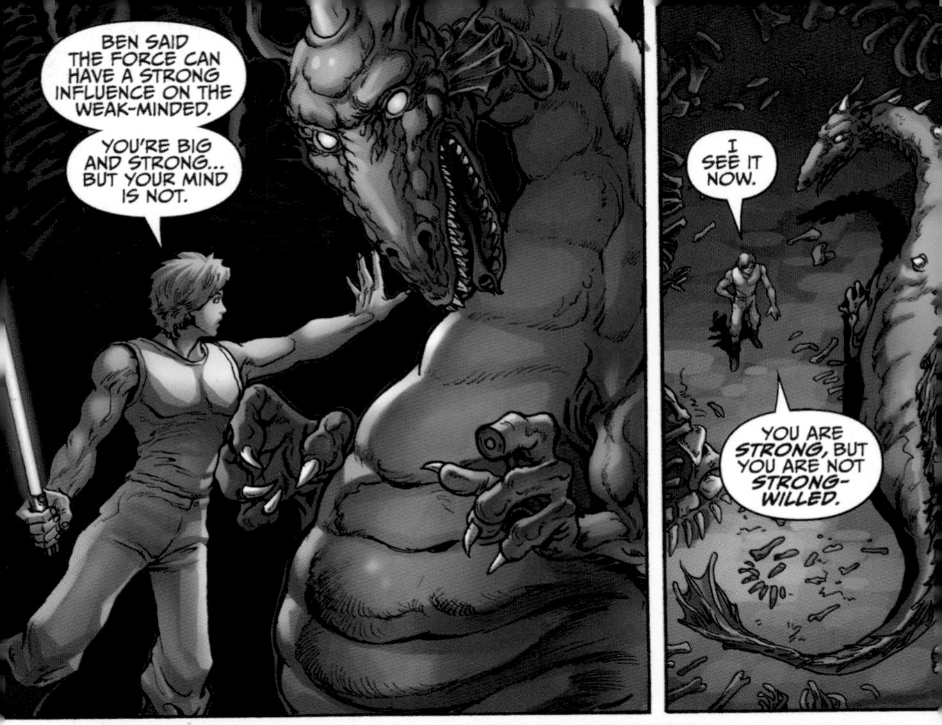

BEN SAID THE FORCE CAN HAVE A STRONG INFLUENCE ON THE WEAK-MINDED.
YOU'RE BIG AND STRONG... BUT YOUR MIND IS NOT.
I SEE IT NOW.
YOU ARE **STRONG,** BUT YOU ARE NOT **STRONG-WILLED.**

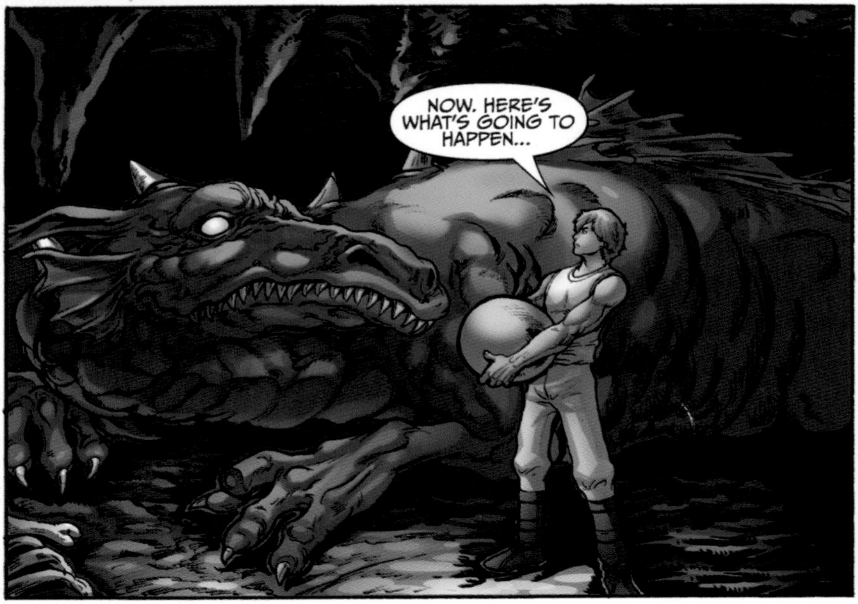

NOW. HERE'S WHAT'S GOING TO HAPPEN...

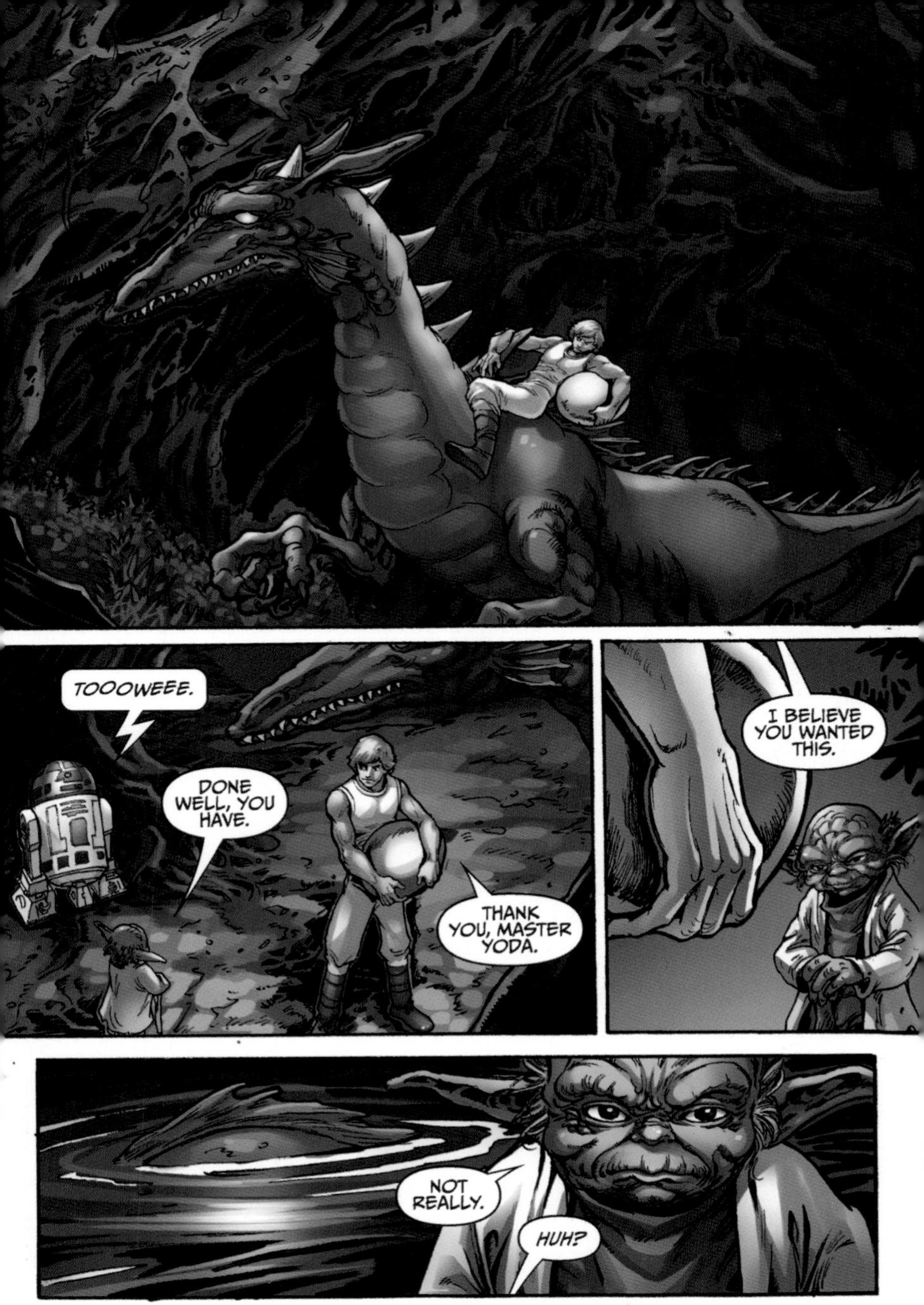
TOOOWEEE.
DONE WELL, YOU HAVE.
THANK YOU, MASTER YODA.
I BELIEVE YOU WANTED THIS.
NOT REALLY.
HUH?

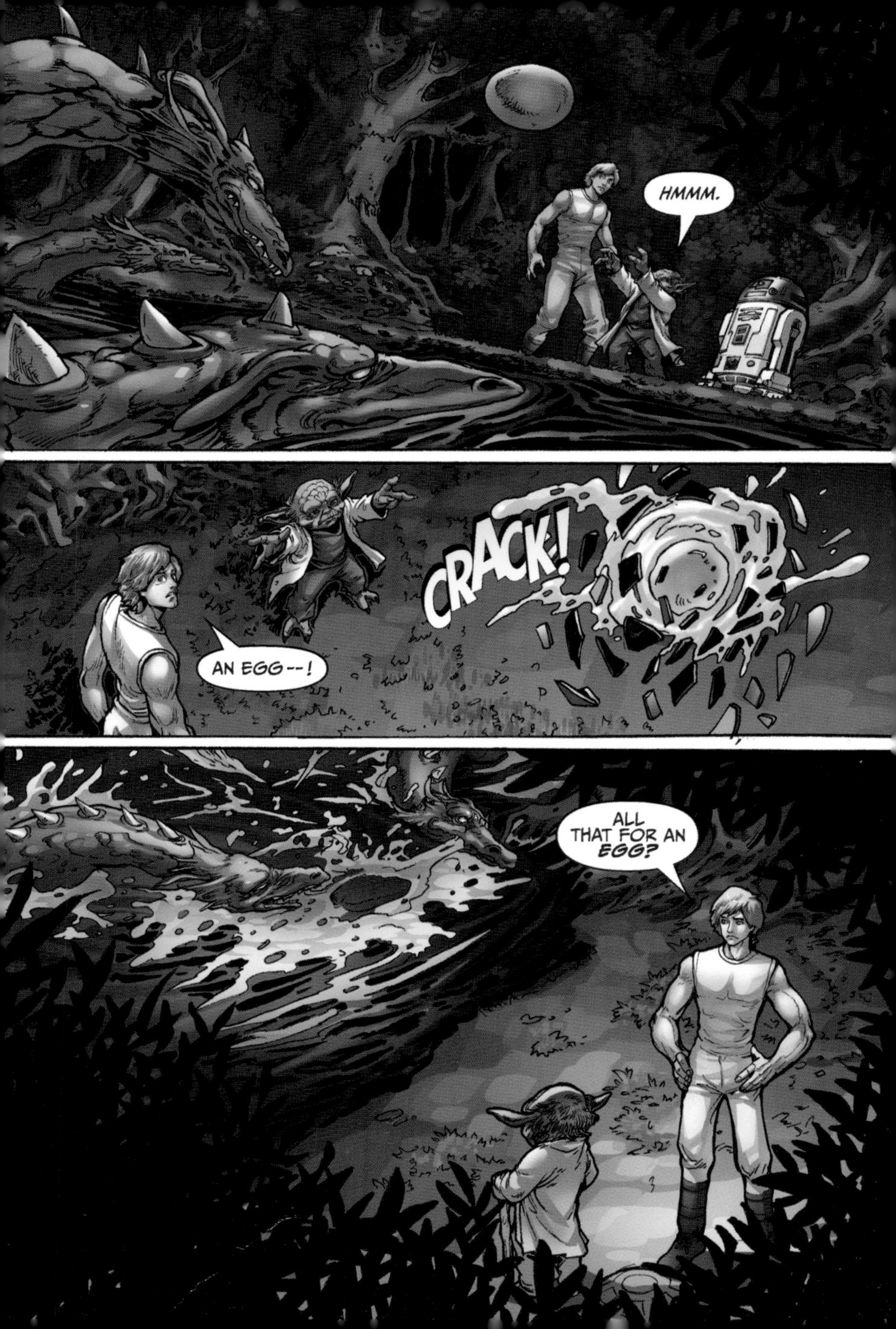
HMMM.
CRACK!
AN EGG--!
ALL THAT FOR AN EGG?

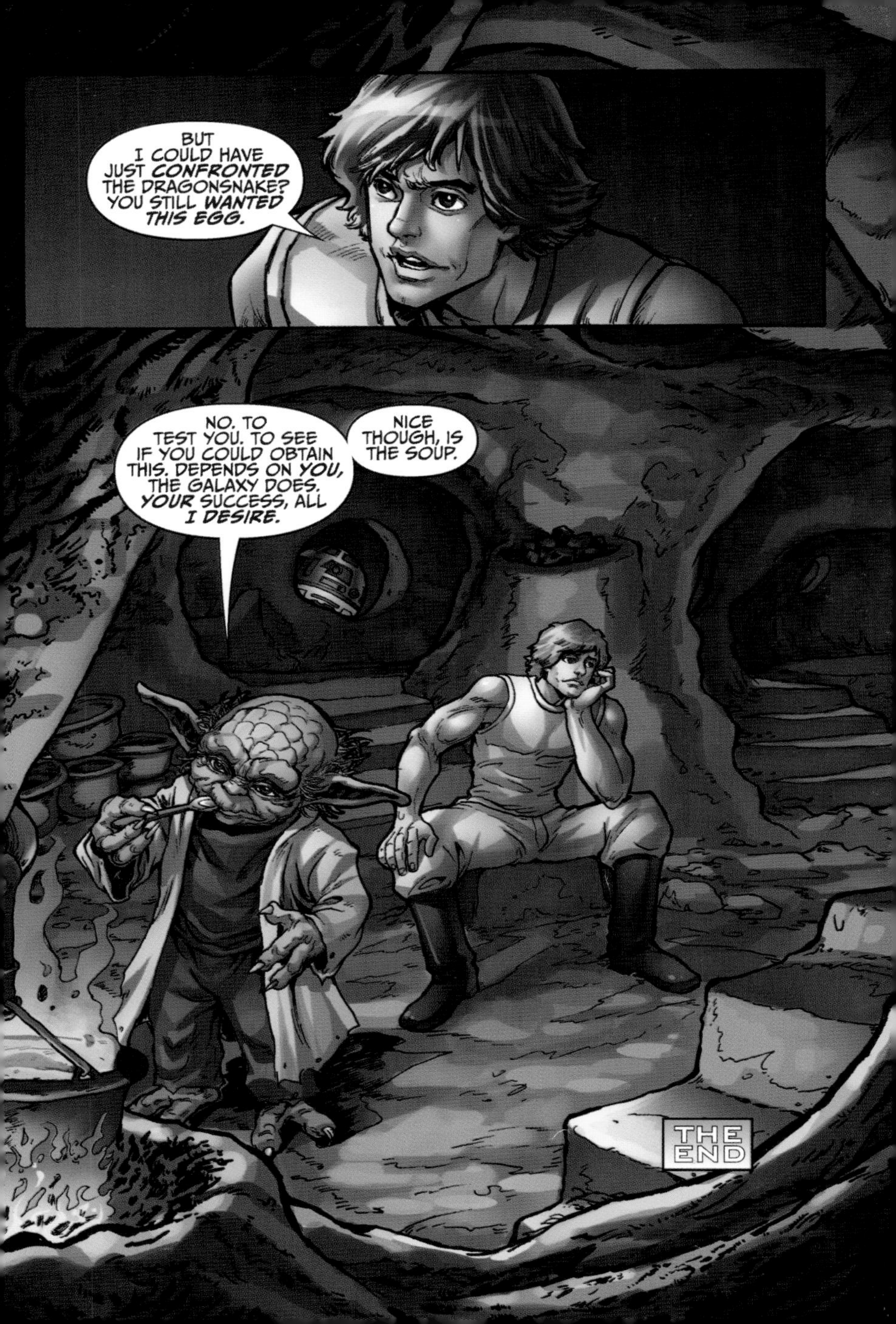
BUT I COULD HAVE JUST CONFRONTED THE DRAGONSNAKE? YOU STILL WANTED THIS EGG.
NO. TO TEST YOU. TO SEE IF YOU COULD OBTAIN THIS. DEPENDS ON YOU, THE GALAXY DOES. YOUR SUCCESS, ALL I DESIRE.
NICE THOUGH, IS THE SOUP.
THE END